ACTS OF CHARITY
ACT ONE

BAYBE
& ME

BY
BEATRICE JAMES

First published in Great Britain in 2015 by:

OBILIUM Ltd
Manchester House - 113 Northgate Street
Bury St Edmunds - IP33 1HP
ISBN 978-1-909868-74-8

*For those who are
struggling for a way out
of an abusive relationship.*

Foreword

Baybe & Me is the first Act of Volume 3 of the 'RETRIBUTION FANTASIES' series. It's a Novella in its own right, however it does follow, sequentially, the first two Volumes of the series.

'AN ARTIST'S IMPRESSION' - Volume One
'SENTENCE EXPIRY DATE' - Volume Two
'ACTS OF CHARITY' 1; 2; 3 & 4 – Volume Three

If you haven't read any of the previous Volumes yet, it may spoil your enjoyment, should you wish to read them later. You can read previews of them all at:

www.BeatriceJames.com

If you have already enjoyed reading the previous books in the series, then we hope that you will be equally pleased by:
'BAYBE & ME'

Acknowledgements

Thank you to:

Jill Baker; Simon & Yvonne Mitchell;

Chris Chatten; Bengi Yuceer & Jane Foong

All at Obilium, for their continued support and patience.

'Man may have discovered fire, but
women discovered how to play with it'

- Candace Bushnell

1

Lizzie
30/12/1994

E lizabeth Forster felt sick. She didn't know if it was nerves, or the two glasses of sherry Terry's mother had forced her to drink. Mrs Mac was a force to be reckoned with and the last thing Lizzie had felt like at ten in the morning was a schooner of Harvey's Bristol Cream.

"Drink up darling, it's your special day." Mrs Mac smiled, showing several missing teeth and the rest stained a nicotine yellow. She meant well, thought Lizzie, but she went through life like a tornado. She had two cleaning jobs and when she wasn't cleaning to earn a crust, she was cleaning at home because she loved to clean. Terry liked things to be clean too. He was used to his mother's ways and had been raised to appreciate a shiny surface and a toilet you could eat your dinner off.

Lizzie knew that with Mrs Mac she had a hard act to follow. Terry was her only child and to say he was the light of her life would be the biggest understatement of 1994. When Lizzie first visited the small terrace house in an unremarkable street in Leytonstone, she knew that it meant the relationship was going places. Terry told her she was the first girl he'd taken home and as he hugged her outside the house, she felt special; she felt loved. Mrs Mac, wearing one of her many overalls, with a flowery print, welcomed her in.

'Perhaps it was her Sunday one?' Lizzie thought as she was ushered in to the spotless living room, overfilled with floral sofas and hundreds of ornaments. Lizzie tried to think nice thoughts and banish the voice in her head that was saying 'how common' and ridiculing her sense of décor and the cheap and nasty china.

She thought of her own living room at home in Edinburgh. 'Tasteful' was the word she would have used. Gold damask chairs, a Chesterfield sofa and bookshelves, built around two walls, reaching to the ceiling. The study with its oak desk and comfortable seats and the room she used to do her homework in, with the radio playing in the corner.

Sickness rose in her throat again as she gulped back a tear. She should have invited her parents today. They hadn't done anything wrong; not really. They had tried too hard to be the perfect parents throughout her life, that's all. The young Elizabeth should have guessed sooner in her life that she probably came from a house like this one. Or maybe worse still, one like the flats behind Terry's pub. She had always felt that something wasn't quite right. A look or a glance between her mother Grace and her father Gerry. There were always secrets, in hushed tones.

Lizzie looked in the cheap gilt mirror in Mrs Mac's hallway. She saw a young woman who looked like she was about to go into surgery, not a girl on the happiest day of her life. Her lustrous red hair seemed to straggle down her back, her green eyes looked tired and the circles under her eyes were exaggerated by the harsh light. Gerry and Grace were both tall and fair. She should have realised a long time ago, she wasn't part of the same gene pool. They'd been gentle when they finally told her. She had been fifteen, a difficult age and she already had enough to deal with. Her hormones were rushing through her body and she had a propensity to cry at the slightest thing. She had looked back at them both as they stared at her earnestly, wanting her to understand, willing her to. They were serious people. There wasn't a lot of laughter in that house. She couldn't imagine how they had summoned up the energy to go through an adoption. Grace must have been at least forty and Gerry older. She was sixty now.

Lizzie had always wondered what it must be like to have a young mum. Someone with energy, vitality and a zest for life. Some of her school friends had younger parents, but the middle class area she lived in, favoured an older 'yummy mummy' and teenage pregnancy was for the lower classes. Lizzie had seen some sights in Leytonstone High Road that reinforced that view. Dark and light skinned girls with long manicured nails and the shortest skirts, bare legged, pushing buggies as if they were trophies. Laughing and smoking, seeing no problem with signing on and spending hours at the council offices, nagging for a flat.

Lizzie despised them, but she didn't know why. They didn't do her any harm, she just felt sorry for their children. The snotty, grimy kids who could hold a Greggs sausage roll before they could walk. What hope did they have? And yet she envied them too. The smallness of their lives. Who had upset who? Their petty arguments and their futile squabbles. What did they have to do all day? Not play with their kids that was for sure. They were too busy shopping, gossiping, drinking and smoking to be too worried about the kids. Perhaps Grace had done her a favour. Her real mother was probably one of 'those young girls,' who hadn't cared enough to keep her baby. Did she need to get back on the game, to buy wraps of heroin?

Edinburgh was a city of contrast and Lizzie had come from the right side of the tracks, but the underbelly of the city was dark and dangerous. Lizzie had often fantasised about her true origins, but she hadn't romanticised the thoughts. Lizzie was a 'glass half-empty' girl. She sank into a depression thinking about her 'birth mother.' What a stupid term. She hadn't tried to find her though. Grace and Gerry had asked her if she wanted to and even offered to help.

'No!' Lizzie was emphatic. 'Leave it be, she didn't want me. Why should I waste my time?'

Over the following months she didn't change her mind, but something changed within her. She couldn't explain it to herself or to her friends and was in a trance like state most of the time. She took her GCSE exams, without any real conviction and got through with passable grades, but her heart wasn't in it. She looked at her friends with their comfortable lives and envied their sense of security. Hers had evaporated along with the love she thought she felt for Gerry and Grace.

Lizzie saw her parents differently now. Everything they said and did annoyed her. Gerry cracking his hardboiled egg in the morning as he read the Independent. 'Tap, tap, tap.' Grace nibbling her dry toast. Lizzie looked at her mother and realised she was verging on anorexic, she ate so little. Lizzie pushed her scrambled egg around the plate and wondered how she could get away before the place consumed her.

Before she knew about the adoption, she felt that her life was her fate. It would be dull like her parents life, but safe. She would go to University like her parents, maybe study English or Politics. Get a sensible job and live the life of a good citizen of Scotland. She knew her place. But it all changed on the day they told her and that life wasn't real anymore.

Lizzie had a talent. Since she had been a little girl she found she could sing. Her voice, as she got older, was rich. It could melt butter. Older than her years, she amazed her relatives whenever she sang for them at family gatherings. Gerry played piano and she would belt out 'Summertime' or 'Love letters' and other old favourites she liked. She wasn't very tall and the voice that came from the slight figure was immense and joyful. Pop, blues, ballads, she could sing anything that people wanted to hear. Lizzie loved to sing. It allowed her to let out some of the feelings she kept locked inside. She didn't want to sing for a living though. Best of all she liked to sing for herself.

On her Seventeenth birthday Lizzie left Scotland. She left Gerry and Grace in a state of shock and then despair, when she told them she wasn't finishing her 'Highers,' she was going to London. Lizzie surprised herself by enjoying the pain she was inflicting upon her parents. It felt good. She wanted to punish them, she didn't know who she was anymore and she placed the blame at their feet.

They begged and pleaded with her to change her mind. Her father got angry, although it wasn't his style. She remembered he called her ungrateful. That had hurt. What had she to be grateful for? She argued. She hadn't asked to be adopted. Did they think they'd done her a favour? It reinforced her decision to go. Her mother cried and hugged her. She felt her small frame wracking with emotion and for a moment almost changed her mind. Lizzie decided she couldn't stay in this prison any more, she needed to find herself. Her mind was made up, she was going to stay with a friend, but would phone them every day.

Fiona, whose parents had moved to London a few months ago, told her there was plenty of room. She was at college doing her 'A' levels and Lizzie could register there too. Lizzie surprised her when she said she wanted to get a job. Grace and Gerry were horrified. It wasn't what they wanted for their little girl. She tried to reassure them she would be with Fiona and her family, not on the streets.

After three hours of Grace and Gerry trying to change her mind, she called a taxi to take her to Waverley Station and left. It made her feel grown up somehow. She felt as if she was in a dream scene again. It was a film that kept playing over and over while she was on the train. She had a small suitcase, a holdall and that was it, but it was freedom and she would survive and make a life for herself.

Her grandmother the ancient matriarch Edith Forster had left her a small inheritance. Luckily she hadn't made it payable upon her twenty first or eighteenth birthday. It was a few thousand pounds, but enough to allow her the luxury of settling into London life. It was 1993, she had the world at her feet. She didn't intend to live the dull life that her mother had chosen.

She had her Walkman on, as she sat back in her seat on the train. It was hard not to sing along to the tracks, she always had to make a conscious effort. The Scorpions belted out 'Wind of change' and she smiled to herself for the first time in a long time. She would have adventures and show Gerry and Grace she didn't need them. She would stand on her own two feet.

It would all be okay.

2

Terry
30/12/1994

M y suit feels amazing. Mum was right as always. Doubled breasted with a looser jacket. Grey with a fleck of something. Pale blue shirt, nice red tie I look the dog's bollocks. In my prime, I would say. A tasty geezer even if I say so myself. Good job I took mum's advice and got my hair cut yesterday. She reminded me I would look at those photos for many years to come. I can admire myself in peace this morning. No mum to nag me, just the sound of Barry in the shower getting ready for the day.

Let's not talk about last night. It was my last night of freedom and let's say I made the most of it. I'm not proud of myself, but hey 'what goes on in The Fox, stays in The Fox.' That's a pub I won't be taking Lizzie to again for a while, that's for sure. Barry and I had had a skinful by then, but it wasn't enough to prevent me from giving Tina the barmaid 'one,' in the back room. I knew she was gagging for it, she'd been giving me the eye for weeks and it was my last chance to do anything about it. I will never be unfaithful to Lizzie, you get it? Never.

I can hear the phone ringing in the hall and know it'll be mum, checking that I'm ready. The taxi will be here in a few minutes. I know her too well. She likes to be in control. Keeping all the balls in the air. I answer it and reassure her it's all going to plan. Lizzie is with her, she stayed the night before the wedding. I won't talk to her though, it's bad luck. Mum says she looks a treat, the hairdresser's just left.

When she asks me what I did last night, I have the decency to cough and she doesn't push it. Years of

17

dealing with my old man have taught her well. She is very understanding my mum.

Despite the slight hangover I feel and look great. I didn't think I would get married so young, but it feels right. Lizzie is the one for me. They say you know when you meet 'the one' and it's true. She rocks my world. She loves me and would do anything for me. What man could ask for more?

Barry and I get in the cab.

"No expense spared," joked Bazza. He's not too impressed with our budget wedding, I can tell.

"Look mate, it ain't all about placemats and bloody gift lists, I just want to marry my bird and live my life."

Barry smiled. "Yeah she is a cracker Tel. Mind you, that didn't stop you last night, you dirty bastard."

Why did he have to say that? My mood changed and I grabbed him by the throat.

"Keep your fucking mouth shut, okay Bazza me old mate." I spat in his face. I was so close to him.

He looked shocked, I'll give him that. Perhaps he had forgotten who he was dealing with. I needed more respect than that.

"Sorry Tel," he stuttered. I laughed and the atmosphere changed.

"Come on mate," I said to the driver, looking at us both, wondering whether to call the Police.

"I've got a wedding to get to."

3

Lizzie
1993

L izzie felt lost. She had left the insular world of Edinburgh, her school, her home and her family and replaced it with a metropolis she didn't understand, or feel part of. Arriving at Kings Cross Station she felt the enormity of what she'd done and some of her earlier excitement had turned to anxiety. The place was heaving with people, coming and going with cases and bags. Couples greeting and others saying their goodbyes. As passengers rushed past her she felt panicky. Then she saw Fiona, coming towards her. She saw the bright yellow top and leggings before she saw Fiona herself. They hugged and both talked at the same time. Fiona was a giant and a willowy five feet eleven, compared to Lizzie's five feet four. She looked well 'wholesome' thought Lizzie. You could tell she was from a good family. Lizzie was now obsessed with 'breeding,' since she found out hers was questionable.

Fiona hailed a cab outside the station. Lizzie thought they would go on the tube. Disappointed, she asked Fiona how it was all going. Did she like London? Fiona loved London. She loved her new school in Kensington near the family home. It was 'all fabulous' and Lizzie noticed that her Edinburgh accent had become more London in a few short months. Fiona asked Lizzie why she had left home. Was she mad? Lizzie told her about her plans to get a job. Fiona looked aghast. "Doing what?"

"I don't know," said Lizzie, realising how she hadn't got a firm plan.

"Well don't worry you can stay with us 'til you get yourself sorted out." Fiona smiled, thinking that Lizzie would be back home in two weeks or so. She couldn't survive here on her own, it was too expensive. She'd soon find that out and be back on the train, with her bags and a good deal of humility.

They pulled up at the house in Kensington and Fiona paid the driver. Lizzie had been to London's museums and the theatres a few times with Grace and Gerry, so she knew this was an affluent area. She remembered coming to the Science museum when she was younger and Gerry was talking about how expensive London was. The house was a three story affair. Painted white, as was the whole terrace, the huge black front door opened as they climbed the steps. Lizzie recognised Caroline, Fiona's mother. She hugged Lizzie as she entered the hallway and Lizzie caught a waft of 'Eau de Temps.'

As they sat sipping tea in the large kitchen. Lizzie realised that Caroline thought she had come for a visit. Fiona gave her 'the look' and she knew not to say anything. As her friend's mother left the room, she looked at Fiona who sighed and said.

"Look Lizzie, I couldn't tell her you have left home. She would freak and be on the phone to your parents in a second. She'll get used to you being here. Give her time. I know how to get round her."

Lizzie wasn't so sure. Good girls from good families didn't just run away to London. She wondered how long it would be before her parents were on the phone and Caroline was 'encouraging' her to go home. This wasn't the 'adventure' she had planned. This would be too much like home. She would stay a few nights then find herself somewhere to live. She had more than enough for a deposit.

While Fiona was at school, next day, Lizzie trudged around looking for somewhere to live. After spending time gazing at the premium rates of the estate agents, she soon realised that the area was far too expensive for her. She gulped at some of the prices, thinking her savings wouldn't last six months if she paid those rents. Even a room in a shared house was out of reach of her budget. She didn't know where to look, her visits as a tourist weren't helping and she realised she didn't know the real London at all.

After two nights at Fiona's she was restless and went on the cleaner's advice. Clarissa was a large black lady who cleaned every morning after the family left for work and school. She was from Homerton in the East end of London and suggested to Lizzie to look for somewhere that side of the city, maybe Wanstead or Woodford.

Clarissa had her own small cleaning company with her 'ladies,' but liked to do the West End herself. Her mother was from Jamaica and she could slip into the lingo, at will. She made Lizzie laugh and she felt comfortable enough to ask her if she had any jobs. Clarissa laughed, deep and loud.

"Oh my god, have you ever done any cleaning? Look at your nails," she chortled. Lizzie looked embarrassed at first, but ended up laughing with her as she told her, her only employment in the past had been a work experience at a local kennels. She confessed to Clarissa that she also hated cleaning.

"You sound perfect girl." Clarissa was still laughing as she drove away in her little pink van. She had promised her she would ask around her friends and neighbours and see if anyone was looking for a 'posh scot' girl who liked to sing.

The following day Lizzie took to public transport and explored the East End. Well the Essex end, she took the central line and got off at Wanstead. A quick look around the green and the shops, including the charming estate agent who told her all she needed to know. It was still too expensive. Jason the estate agent, warned her about certain areas, telling her they weren't safe, too much crime, gangs and robberies. He suggested she try Leyton, Leytonstone, or Walthamstow. Solid, working class areas, but not too expensive or 'dodgy.' She was learning, slowly and thanked him for his help.

At the crossroads near Wanstead Station there was a pub on the corner. It was advertising cheap lunches and Lizzie realised how hungry she was, after walking around for what seemed like hours. She went in and ordered a shepherd's pie and an orange juice and sat at a seat near the window.

A few minutes later a group of three males sauntered into the Pub. They were wearing some kind of army trousers with lots of pockets and knee pads and big jackets over their jumpers and T-shirts. Builders, she guessed, noticing the youngest one of the three. He wasn't tall, five nine or ten, but taller than her at least. Well-built with strong shoulders and arms, she noticed his bright blue eyes and cheeky grin. He had short dark hair and was the most handsome man she thought she had ever seen. In a working class kind of way, she thought to herself, looking down at her food, her appetite fading.

She couldn't stop looking at him as he stood up at the bar drinking a pint of something. 'They shouldn't be drinking if they are working?' She wondered why she was so obsessed with what he was doing. He was just a good looking guy she'd never see again.

The men ordered cheese rolls and crisps and she caught his eye. Or at least he caught her looking at him. He smiled at her and winked. Her heart did a somersault and she wondered if he'd speak to her. She wasn't sure she could say anything if he did. Her mouth was dry so she took a sip of her orange juice, then took out the Estate Agent's sheets with the details of the local properties.

She pretended to read, feeling a bit stupid. 'Get a grip,' she told herself.

4

Terry
1993

I saw her as soon as we got into the pub. Me, Barry and Jake had a break and I needed a pint and some grub. We had been working on a place in Overton Drive. A contract job building an extension. I had started at eight and was ready for a break. We'd been in 'The Bull' pub twice that week and it was a decent pint and food if you wanted it.

There she was, sitting in the corner; small build, the way I like them. Long red hair and a fringe and big eyes. I couldn't see the colour, but big, gorgeous eyes. Tight jeans and boots, another favourite of mine. I watched her out of the corner of my eye and saw her looking at me. I gave her the full Terry treatment, the big smile and the wink. She almost winced, it made my day. I don't like noisy brash birds, they piss me off. She looked classy.

I've never had a problem with confidence that's for sure, but I didn't want to frighten her off. She looked like she was a shy one. I waited a few minutes then tried my luck. She was reading something looked like some Estate Agent's blurb. Perhaps she was looking for a house. She didn't look like she was short of a bob or two. Young though, maybe eighteen or nineteen. The right age for me, a horny twenty year old. I was on the lookout after that bitch Laura gave me the heave-ho.

I remember walking up to her table, cool as a polar bear on a winter's day. Okay I wasn't dressed in my finest threads, but some birds like the 'rough' workman look, if you get my meaning. She looked up from whatever she was reading. It's weird, but I can remember her eyelashes they were long and made those beautiful eyes even more attractive. My opening gambit was, "you looking for somewhere to live, luv?"

She smiled and said, "you must be a detective?"

Weird accent, I thought, could be Scottish, but posh Scottish. I wondered if she was being sarky.

I flashed the Terry smile again and sat down next to her. She flinched as I remember.

"You're jumpy babe. What's the matter? Are the Old Bill after you?"

She laughed now and I could see her relax. She told me her name was Lizzie and she'd moved from Edinburgh to London a few days ago and was staying in Kensington.

I have to admit I was very attracted by her. She wasn't like the usual girls I meet. She was quiet and had class, I liked that. I ramped up the Terry charm and looked straight into her eyes as we spoke. I gave her the usual spiel about me. The edited version if you like. Told her about my old man leaving my mum when I was fourteen. Got himself a Thai bride. Broke my mum's heart. I went watery-eyed at this point. For my mum, not the old bastard.

She looked at me. I knew I had her. She took hold of my hand. What a sweetheart I remember thinking.

"I'm so sorry Terry." She looked upset herself bless her.

I was just getting to know more about her when Barry and Jake called me over to go back to work. It would have been easy to just get up and go, give her my phone number and hope she would ring. That was my usual way. 'Treat 'em mean, keep 'em keen,' you know what I mean, but something stopped me, I wanted this girl and I didn't want her getting away and forgetting me.

Telling her to wait, I went up to the boys at the bar and told Barry to tell the boss, mum was ill and I had to go home. He looked puzzled.

"When did she ring you?" He asked.

I'd just got a new phone, a mobile Nokia and thought it was well cool.

"She didn't, you stupid bastard, I'm staying right here. Me and Lizzie will be getting to know each other better and get used to it Bazza, 'cause that little lady will be my wife one day."

Where the fuck had that come from, I wondered afterwards. Mum had told me it was my subconscious, but I don't believe in all that crap. Let's say I just knew and leave it at that.

I knew the next couple of hours were crucial. I persuaded her to have a vodka in her orange juice, the landlord wasn't paying much attention and she could pass for eighteen. That loosened her up and she told me all about her parents and being adopted and all that. I thought she was making a fuss about nothing if you ask me. She was lucky not to be brought up by the woman who birthed her. I'm guessing she was poor or underage or both, but I could tell she was upset, so I made all the right noises.

"Oh babe, that must have been tough for you."

Us men know what to say when we need to. Just takes effort. I'm not great at listening, my mum would tell you that, but I made a real effort. Mixed up and emotional, she needed someone like me to take care of her.

After two more drinks she said she needed to get back to Kensington. I took her to the tube.

"Are you going be okay babe?"

She nodded. She looked happier than when I first saw her. That's the 'Terry effect' mind you. Works every time.

I made some calls before we left and spoke to two landlords I'd done some work for. One had a property off Leytonstone High road, not far from my house.

'Fucking perfect,' I thought to myself. I'll meet her at Leytonstone Station, tomorrow morning at eleven. Lucky it was Saturday, so I didn't have to put my job on the line by taking another day off. She looked so pleased. I kissed her. I wasn't rough; it was a lover's kiss. We'd be lovers soon, I knew that for a fact and I'd leave her wanting more.

I certainly wanted more.

5

Lizzie

L izzie held her breath as he approached. She couldn't believe her luck. He looked even more handsome in the light of the bay window she was sitting in. Dark close cropped hair, those bright blue eyes focussed on her and that smile. It made her weak at the knees. She didn't want him to speak in a way. It would spoil the illusion. He was a Greek God. Those muscles and his chest moving underneath the tight T-shirt; it's a macho thing. It wasn't that warm in the pub and she could see his nipples.

She tried to focus as he asked her the question, 'was she looking for somewhere to live?' He didn't look like a landlord. He couldn't have been much older than her. She looked down at the Estate Agent's material and couldn't resist asking him if he was a detective? She still wasn't sure what his angle was. He sat down next to her and close enough for their legs to touch. She flinched. She could feel the heat from him, or was she imagining it?

He told her she was jumpy and asked if the Police were after her. It melted the frost. They laughed together. He had a sexy accent she decided. Cockney yes, but with a slight raspiness to his voice he said came from smoking too much. He offered her a cigarette, she politely refused. He asked if she minded if he smoked. She didn't. He could have set himself on fire, as long as he stayed where he was and looked at her in the way he was doing.

No one had showed her as much interest as this ever, not even the spotty boys at her school. He was a man, but his boyish looks told her he was not that much older than her, which was true.

He was twenty and said his name was Terence. 'Terry' to his mates; named after Terence Stamp, his mother's favourite actor. He told her about his mum, who, after trying for a baby for years, finally had him when she was thirty two. He told her about his dad, who left when he was fourteen. His mum found out he had been having an online affair for eighteen months with a Thai woman called Pim. He left to move there and set up home with his Thai Bride. Lizzie was pleased he was telling her all this. He got upset when he told her about his dad, her heart went out to him and she took his hand. He was so sensitive. She felt she had found a soul mate.

His mates were going and he said he would stay. She didn't question him. She wanted him to stay. He bought her a couple of vodkas and soon she told him her story. She found him easy to talk to. He really seemed to understand how she felt. How lucky was it she had come into this pub on this day? Lizzie often wondered about fate. She would think more about it in years to come. They were destined to meet, she was sure of it. He even offered to phone some landlords to help her find a place. He set one up to see the following day and they met at the Underground Station. She had never been to Leytonstone, but it sounded so romantic. Eleven o'clock tomorrow; it was a date.

Lizzie felt happier than she could remember feeling for months, years even. She had such a good feeling about Terry. As they approached Wanstead tube, he pulled her to him. He kissed her in a way that was passionate yet tender at the same time. Lizzie had been kissed before, but never like this. He smelt of tobacco and aftershave. His arms felt strong and protective and she felt the warmth of his embrace on that cold afternoon like a blanket around her. He pulled away and they smiled at each other. Then he was kissing her again and she didn't want it to stop.

6

Terry

L izzie had a mobile phone, her parents had insisted on it when she left. It seemed modern for Scotland, but it was handy that she had one too. We exchanged numbers outside the station and believe it or not, mobiles were not all that great in 1993. Those Nokias weren't smart phones at all, it makes me laugh to think about them now. But useful, oh yes. I have never been good with words so it's far easier to text than to say things. After we made arrangements to meet next day and I left Lizzie, I waited an hour then sent a message to her.

'Babe. It was great to meet you. Can't wait til tomorrow, I've never talked to anyone in the way I talked to you. xxxxx'

And so on and so forth. Easy really and I meant what I was saying. She was different. Pure and unspoilt. Funny, but serious. She had 'the hots' for me and she brought out the best in me. Well in the beginning anyway.

I saw her at the tube station. She had a big green scarf wrapped around her shoulders and the leather jacket she had worn yesterday. Same jeans and boots and I guessed she had brought little down from Scotland with her. She was freezing until I warmed her up with a bear hug and the kind of kiss that usually leads straight to my bed. I went for tongues I think she was ready. She needed to know she was with a hot blooded male. I felt myself get hard and wished that I could've had her right there. She didn't realise the effect she was having on me and was chattering away about the flat.

I had the keys. I'd picked them up from Sanjay on the way to meet Lizzie. It was a one bedroomed flat, a conversion on the top floor of one of the older style houses. It had a kitchen and bathroom and was cheap for the area. Sanjay owed me a favour and he agreed to let it for four hundred a month if Lizzie wanted it. I knew it would need some work knowing Sanjay. He wasn't known in Leytonstone for his luxury apartments. I held Lizzie's arm and we walked up the High Road together. Her cheeks were flushed and she looked beautiful. I hoped the place was unfurnished, or I might have to persuade her to try out the bed before she takes the place. There was something about her youth, her eagerness to please that turned me on. The girls around her were mouthy and cheap and liked to be in charge. They weren't the girls for me.

We turned off the main drag into Ashen Drive then off that was Bailey Road. The flat was half way along on the left and I told Lizzie she could get to the tube in minutes, once she got a job. We went up the steps together and I opened the front door. The lobby was grubby and smelly and I could see her nostrils flaring. Bless her, she wasn't used to slumming it. I joked with her she would have to drop her standards if she wanted to live in London. We climbed the stairs past flats B and C, to the top floor. There was a flat on each floor, so she wouldn't have to share the landing with anyone and would have her own front door. The stairs going up to the flat were steep, but I told her it would keep her fit. Especially if she was carrying shopping.

The flat had been empty for two or three months according to Sanjay. Although he hadn't realised that the tenants had moved out. He knew they owed rent and kept trying to catch them to sort it out. A few days ago he opened the door with his own keys and found they had done a runner.

The door opened straight into the lounge, which seemed a fair size, but I don't know what her house in Scotland's like. Maybe it's a fucking mansion. Off the lounge was a small kitchenette. I looked at Lizzie to see her reaction. She didn't look appalled, which was good. The kitchen was manky with leftover food and bottles all over it. The foul smell was coming from a litter tray that still appeared to have its cat's droppings in. God some people live like pigs I told her.

The bedroom was off the lounge and had a nice bay window. The fleeing tenants had left a double bed and a sad looking sofa in the front room. Apart from their rubbish that was all they had left. Still I told Lizzie, the kitchen had a cooker and fridge so it could be worse. She agreed. I pulled her towards me and she relaxed into my arms. Trust that was all it took. I whispered into her ear.

"I'll make it nice for you babe. Give me a week and I will show you what I can do." She smiled at me. I'm not a tall geezer, but I felt about six foot that day.

Lizzie was looking at me with hope and excitement in her eyes. This was her new home and I was her new knight in shining armour. Her 'hero,' as she would sing to me on our wedding day. She sang it better than Mariah Carey.

7

Lizzie

He didn't disappoint. After a sleepless night at Fiona's in the spare bedroom, she went over and over their meeting and the things he had said. Perhaps she was being naïve believing it all. He had sent her some texts after they parted and she felt she had made the right decision trusting Terry. He was reliable and romantic. She blushed at some things he said to her. She was still a virgin, but she didn't want him to know that.

A few weeks ago she had been a stupid schoolgirl. She was an independent woman now. She wanted him to see her like that. He made her feel like a woman when he touched her and she wanted more. When she saw him coming towards her at the tube, she forgot her annoyance that he was half an hour late, she was so pleased to see him. He had the keys to a flat. He was a miracle. She had been so lost in London, and alone. Now she had the possibility of a home and a relationship. It was all good.

The flat wasn't quite what she expected. It was smaller than she had hoped for, but it was near to the tube, as Terry pointed out, for when she'd got a job and travelling to earn her own living. The lounge was okay, but the bedroom was her favourite room, with a bay window overlooking the street and was bright and sunny. She grimaced at the kitchen and bathroom. Terry explained that the tenants had left 'in a hurry' so the place hadn't had a proper clean.

The kitchen made her feel sick, because of the cat's litter tray. Terry had been so sweet telling her he would sort it out for her to move in the following weekend. She was so lucky to have found him. He was a gem.

The next few days went by quickly for Lizzie. Terry seemed to take charge of everything. They went to see Sanjay and she signed the tenancy agreement. It felt such a grown up thing to do. Six months to start with, but it could be extended. Terry had negotiated a cheaper rent and she wrote a cheque to Sanjay for the deposit and the first month's rent. She would need to buy things for the place, but she still had the bulk of her inheritance left so she wasn't too worried. When she told Terry she'd had money left to her, he didn't seem interested, saying she wouldn't need much, once he'd sorted the place out. He told her to wait outside whilst he spoke to Sanjay and she guessed he was arranging for the place to be cleaned.

After they left Sanjay's place Terry told her he was taking her 'up West' before she went back to Kensington. It was late afternoon by now and they went for a drink in a pub off Oxford Street to celebrate. He ordered a bottle of Champagne and they toasted her new life. Lizzie felt euphoric. It wasn't just the bubbles. She rang her parents Grace and Gerry and told them she had found a flat. They didn't seem happy for her at all and she felt upset. Terry was sweet and said that they had probably expected her to come home. She could invite them to the flat when she had a job and show them how well she was doing. He was right, they were selfish, they didn't care about what she wanted.

Terry took her for dinner at a nearby steak house. Lizzie wasn't that fond of red meat, but he told her he was a 'steak man' and she liked the fact he knew what he wanted. He ordered for her and she struggled to eat the meat as rare as it was. He told her she could choose where they went next time, but she didn't care as long as he was there. She ate the baked potato and salad and pushed the meat under the lettuce. She didn't want to offend Terry, he had been so good to her.

The following Saturday she left Kensington with the small suitcase she had brought from Edinburgh. Fiona and her mother were upset to see her go, but happy she had found herself somewhere to live. When she told Caroline she was staying in London and moving to Leytonstone she was shocked, as expected. She offered to help, but as Lizzie said, she had little to move. She promised to invite them both over 'for dinner' as soon as she had settled in. Such grown up behaviour. She'd told them about Terry, but had played down how much he'd done. She wanted to retain some kind of independence. As she walked to the underground station she felt she was starting her new life.

8

Terry

Things were working out just sweet. Lizzie took the flat on my advice and I arranged a deal with Sanjay. As part of the favour he owed me, which I won't go into, he agreed to sort out the place and paint the rooms. I persuaded him to get in a cleaning company and he agreed that I would give it the Terry seal of approval on Thursday, before Lizzie moved in on Saturday.

I took her up the West End for a drink and a meal. We had a great dinner at the steakhouse. They all know me there and I think they impressed her with the service. I ordered her a steak with a béarnaise sauce which for me was the height of sophistication. She seemed to enjoy it, but come to think about it, did spend a lot of time chewing! Women eh? We had champagne and things were moving along at a fair pace. She rang her parents, but they clearly weren't happy. Oh well. She won't need them now, she has me to look after her. They are miles away anyway and treat her like a kid.

I went to the flat on Thursday as arranged. Give Sanjay his due he had done a sterling job. He'd had the carpets cleaned and the painters had been in to paint the rooms the old favourite magnolia. The kitchen was spotless and there was no sign of the cat litter tray. He had got rid of the sofa and old bed and replaced them with a new Ikea sofa and a king size bed, all paid for by me. The bed was the most important purchase. I have even got my old mum involved even though she hasn't met Lizzie yet. I sent her to John Lewis to get a duvet and some bedding, some pans and crockery. She even waited in whilst they delivered it. You must think I am mad, spending cash on some bird I've just met. I don't see it like that. It's an investment. An investment in my future, 'cause I will live here soon, given time. Then I can shag her to my heart's content. Women are easily pleased you know. Just takes effort. My old mum is quite intrigued. She has never seen me do anything much for anyone. I did lie and tell her we met a few weeks ago. I didn't want her to think I had lost my marbles. She doesn't have to know everything.

She couldn't help doing the cleaning when she got to the flat. Moaning that 'those industrial cleaners don't do a proper job' getting out her vinegar and lemon juice and the bloody bleach. What a woman. No one calls her by her real name. Weird isn't it? Everyone round here calls her Mrs Mac. I call her mum or queen mum depending what mood she is in. Her actual name is Alice, but she doesn't look like an Alice at all. She still does everything for me. My mates can't believe it and take the piss, something rotten. She even irons my underpants how about that for service. All I have to worry about is getting to work. I see her all right though.

She gets her housekeeping money from me every Friday whatever happens. I told her I don't want her to get herself a boyfriend. Since dad fucked off to Thailand she has been lonely, bless her. She has her mates, but she doesn't go out much. She isn't going to meet anyone at the Bingo now is she? All those women cackling away.

Still she doesn't need a man. I give her enough cash and at least I don't beat the shit out of her like my old man. She has a charmed life apart from all the cleaning jobs, but she likes that. She would go mental if she couldn't clean. When I was a kid I wondered what she was trying to scrub away. Who knows?

Was it all worth it you're asking me? Of course it was. It might have been like a military operation, but it was well worth it. Or so I thought at the time. Hindsight is a wonderful thing so they say. I couldn't have told you how things would work out any more than she could. We had something back then. We both felt it. Her face was a picture when she turned up at the flat. I said I'd meet her at twelve, to give her plenty of time to get there, but I went extra early to add finishing touches.

Good job I'd been watching 'Space Craft' eh? What's that you might say if you were born after the eighties? Look it up. How to turn a couple of rooms into palaces in two days for a few hundred quid. Except they had a designer and I had me and my mum and the painter and the Industrial cleaners. Well it was my idea I suppose.

I took her up the stairs. Sanj had even had the hall, stairs and landing done 'for her ladyship' as he calls her. It was like a different place. It stunk of paint, but hey ho, better than cat shit. The lounge had a nice big sofa for us to cuddle up on and a large sheepskin rug and cushions. Mum had even washed the blinds and curtains. The kitchen when painted red looked a million times better than before. I had hung up the red saucepans and accessories earlier that morning and mum had bought some tea towels. Lizzies face was a picture. Her mouth hung open, she obviously hadn't expected too much.

By the time she reached the kitchen and saw the stuff we'd put in she was crying. She hugged me and kissed me, and even more grateful than I had hoped for. What a result. As we went into the bedroom and she saw the new bedding she was on a cloud. I had gone mad and got some candles on a tray. What woman doesn't like a candle? Psychology, but it worked and oh yes she was grateful.

As I poured out the fizz I'd put in the fridge earlier I knew how the day would pan out. It wouldn't be long before I was pounding my already stiff dick right into her tight virgin passage. She hadn't told me she was a virgin, but I'd worked it out. She hadn't even had a proper boyfriend from what I could make out. Who better to teach her the language of love?

I even smiled to myself at the thought.

9

Lizzie

L izzie was overwhelmed when she met Terry outside the flat. She knew he had been working hard to get the place sorted and she imagined he had arranged for someone to give it a good clean up. Perhaps put a throw on the sofa and sort out that horrible kitchen. She hoped it would be clean enough to move into. She planned to go to a cheap bedding shop she'd passed on the High Road, to pick up a duvet and some bedding. Maybe some cushions and a rug, just to make it more homely.

He hugged her outside the flat and she put down her case, reaching on tip toes as she kissed him. She couldn't believe she had only known this man for two weeks, not even that and look what he had done for her. The change in the flat amazed her, with a new sofa, lovely rug, cream walls, it was all perfect. She cried when she went into the kitchen. Her first kitchen. He had bought pans to match the red paint. Good pans and crockery. Surely the landlord hadn't provided that. It was Terry, her saviour.

The bathroom, cleaned until it shone, had had some toiletries put in it for her to enjoy and 'oh my God, candles, what a man!' She couldn't believe it. The place was ready for her to move into. She followed him into the bedroom and saw the Sun and Moon duvet cover, the new blinds, the freshly painted wardrobe and chest of drawers. It was her own little house and it was in London. All she needed to do now was find a job. She would show her parents and all the doubters, she could survive and make a go of her life.

Terry poured them a glass of champagne. Well, a large glass of fizzy wine. She sipped at her drink, feeling the euphoria of life she hadn't thought she could, during the last couple of years. She looked at her hero. His blue eyes were sparkling as he grinned at her like a Cheshire cat. Terry was pleased that she was pleased, it was as simple as that and it was genuine. He liked her and he wanted to help her sort out her life. Pulling her down onto the bed, he unzipped her jeans. She wasn't sure she was ready for this, but he had done so much. She thought she loved him. Maybe this was love.

She felt his mouth on her nipple and a shudder of desire ran through her body. Soon they were both naked and he was admiring her body as he ran his tongue up and down her until she thought she would scream with utter pleasure. She had her first orgasm whilst his expert mouth was licking her, his hands on her hips so she couldn't move away. She didn't want to.

They drank more 'champagne' and he showed her how to please him. Licking his shaft and his balls until he was about to climax. Then he was gentle, pushing slowly until he was inside her. Sliding back and forth and increasing in tempo, she could feel he was about to burst. He hadn't used a condom, she was thinking as she felt his hot fluid spurt inside her, his rhythmic contractions making her come again.

She lay in his arms feeling content and safe. If this was sex she wanted more of it. He had been so caring, so eager to please, but she needed to go and sort out some contraception now she was with Terry. She hoped he wasn't going anywhere.

Terry had fallen into a deep post coital sleep. He'd been up early and the champagne on an empty stomach had all contributed to his tired state. She looked at him lying next to her. He was magnificent. He was her man. She felt like singing. Music, that what's she needed to get. A CD player with a radio and some speakers. She couldn't live without music. There wasn't a TV, but she wasn't bothered about that she just needed some sounds. Next Lizzie went to the bathroom and tried out the shower, then wrapped herself in the big white towel and went back into the bedroom. Terry was still asleep. He was a heavy sleeper she was finding out. She pulled on some clothes and went to find a supermarket for food and a Hi-Fi shop to buy a cheap CD player. Her phone was next to the bed, she didn't bother taking it as she wouldn't be long.

Leytonstone High Road was a jumble of shops, big and small and some of the places she found were intriguing. Fruit and vegetable shops selling things she had never heard of or seen before. Colourful characters on the small market and the sights and sounds of cosmopolitan London fascinated Lizzie, a girl from the suburbs of Edinburgh.

There were shops selling second hand furniture and after a demonstration, she bought a CD player for twenty pounds including the speakers. She carried it straight back to the flat, because the equipment was heavier than she thought. The food shopping could wait until she went back out later.

Lizzie struggled up the stairs with her new purchase and opened the door to the flat. Terry, now dressed, was sitting on the sofa, staring into space. She smiled at him.

"Hi Terry." She told him she had bought a CD player so they could have some music.

"Where have you been?" His whole demeanour was different. He gave her a cold stare. "We were in bed. You just disappeared."

"But you were asleep." Lizzie didn't understand what she'd done wrong?

"I don't like waking up on my own." All the warmth had gone and he seemed like a stranger. Lizzie felt panicky, she'd thought she was doing the right thing.

"Sorry Terry. I didn't mean to upset you after everything you have done. I just wanted to get us some music."

"I don't care about music." He almost spat the words.

"I do," she said softly, with tears forming in her eyes. She wanted things to be the way they'd been before.

"Ok," he said. "You stay here and I'll go and get us something to eat."

Lizzie started to say she wanted to cook, but the words stuck in her throat. She didn't want to risk annoying him again.

"Oh okay, thanks." He went out without hugging or touching her. After he'd left she burst into tears. She didn't know what had happened.

She waited for him. In silence. She realised she had no CDs to put on the player she had rushed out to get.

He came back four hours later, smelling of beer and smoke. He threw her a package.

"Kebab," he said, slurring his words, then fell asleep on the sofa.

Lizzie wondered what had just happened here. She went to bed leaving Terry on the sofa. A few hours later she woke up to feel him on top of her, pushing his way inside her. He wasn't so gentle this time.

"You're hurting me Terry." She almost cried. He finished, collapsing on her as he did and all she could smell was stale beer.

When she awoke he was making them breakfast as if nothing had happened.

"All right babe? Sorry I was pissed last night. Hope I wasn't too rough." He had showered and he smelt like the old Terry. He nibbled her earlobe and her neck whilst holding on to the frying pan. They ate bacon sandwiches and drank builder's tea, hot and strong, whilst still in bed. Terry pulled her to him and pushed her face down to his cock. She started to suck. He was hard again and inside her within seconds. He was taking his time, taking her with him, as he rotated his cock inside her until they came together. She cried out this time, as her body took over.

Lizzie felt confused and just wanted to feel safe, in the way she had yesterday before his outburst. What she didn't yet know was she would never feel that safe again.

Not really.

10

Terry

There is only one woman in the world who won't let me down, my old mum. I thought that Lizzie was the same, but she isn't. She isn't as perfect as I first thought. The height of her perfection was in our first fuck. The new flat, the new bed, the new Lizzie. We drank two glasses of fizz and she was more than ready. She was grateful and she was wet for me. She was so tight it was bliss. I had been on my best behaviour and hadn't rushed her, I didn't want to spoil her first time. I was proud that I'd made her come twice. In my experience virgins didn't usually come at all. It took a while, but she was well up for it, like a natural.

I couldn't believe it when I woke up and she had gone. Gone where? No note. Nothing. Just slipped out like a thief in the night. What a bitch. I didn't think she was like the others, but they're are all the same underneath. My old man told me that. Mind you he didn't appreciate mum in the way I do. He was quick to turn her in for a new model when the time was right.

I remember him saying she was getting too gobby and answering him back, it was an outrage. She even rang the Police once, when he'd given her a slap. It was the East End way, he told her, to keep her in line. Pissed as a fiddler's bitch at the time, he didn't realise he'd broken her nose.

Back to Lizzie. I wasn't best pleased when she got back and let her know it. I don't want to frighten her off though. She was gutted when she saw how upset I was, silly tart. I keep forgetting how young she is. She could be a keeper, if I mould her in the right way. She is a quick learner that's for sure. When I first met her I thought I might be punching above my weight, but I must have been having a crisis of confidence. She'll stay all right. I gave her a good seeing too last night and showed her who's boss. She can't live without me now. She has no other mates in London and if I have anything to do with it, it'll stay that way. Don't want the mouthy lot round here telling her all about me and my business.

I have an idea. It came to me this morning as I was lying next to her and feeling horny again. I'll take her to meet my mum. She will love Mrs Mac and Mrs Mac will love her. She is desperate to see this girl I've been going to so much trouble for. I won't keep her in suspense any longer and roused Lizzie by rubbing her breast. She murmured and turned toward me. She had a strange look on her face when she opened her eyes. I could have sworn it was fear. What's she got to be afraid about? Perhaps she had a nightmare. Who knows what goes on in the mind of a woman?

"Babe, wake up." She still had that startled look. "Go and make me a cuppa." I gave her my best smile as I kissed her. She got up and came back with a brew, the way I like it. Perhaps she could be forgiven. I pulled her towards me and she relaxed.

"What do you want to do today?" Lizzie asked me. I told her I wanted her to meet mum. She didn't realise how close my mum lived, but then again, I hadn't told her.

"Let's go and have one of mum's roasts babe." She was smiling now. "She doesn't get to meet girlfriends of mine, you realise that Lizzie? You're special, so go and make me some breakfast while I ring her."

Mum was elated, as I'd expected her to be. Her fridge was always stocked and she would have been making a dinner for me anyway. She always did. I go to the Fox for a few pints to get over the night before and then I can face food.

"Mum, we'll come at half one, okay?" Lizzie was back in the room. "Yeah she can't wait to meet you too. See you later."

"Forget the breakfast babe, get over here." She obliged and I pulled off her T-shirt. As I suckled her breasts she was already moaning. 'Putty in my hands,' I thought, 'putty in my hands.'

After a nice little session in the sack. I looked at my watch. "Fuck, it's half eleven." Lizzie looked startled.

"What should I wear Terry?" Which was sweet, wanting to please me and look nice for my mum.

"Haven't you got a dress or something?" I asked her. She produced a black, long-sleeved dress from the suitcase. It was stretchy, but it was decent. It showed off her figure a treat. Small waist and womanly tits and hips.

"Go and shower now," I said, lying back on the bed. It was going to be a good day.

I rang mum back and told her to change the arrangements. We would be there at half two. She was used to my ways. She had a moan, but I took little notice. I would take Lizzie to the Fox first and show her off. She looked a class act in that dress and her high boots. As she emerged from the shower I told her we were going to the pub first.

"I'd better put some make up on then Terry, I want to look at least eighteen." And look eighteen she did. Nearer twenty. I had a quick rinse and a spray of deodorant. Last night's T-shirt would be okay I decided. I didn't want to go home first. We set off together to the pub and she was all smiles now.

11

Lizzie

Lizzie decided that Terry was two different people. There was nice Terry, thoughtful Terry, kind Terry and loving Terry. Then there was the Terry who didn't like to be crossed. She decided she could deal with that. She chided herself for last night. It was good he wanted her so much. She would have to get used to his ways if the relationship was to last. She couldn't imagine life without him now. Nice Terry made her feel good about herself. Warm inside and desirable. The other Terry made her feel useless. A failure. She couldn't have that. She would just have to try harder. After all it was her first real relationship, she had no real experience of men.

At least not men like him. The others, had been boys. A few kisses and gropes at parties. Spotty youths with their hands all over her. Terry knew what he was doing all right and the miracle was he wanted her, Lizzie Forster. Nothing special, boring old Lizzie. Even her own mother hadn't wanted her. She knew she had done the right thing coming to London. It was fate.

When Terry asked if she wanted to meet his mum, she knew it was serious. She knew he never asked anyone else. He was older than her and he must have had loads of girlfriends. He was so good looking. Those eyes and that smile was a killer combination. He could charm the birds from the trees. She was a lucky girl.

As she dressed and put on some makeup, she wanted his approval. He liked the dress. That was a good start. She felt like singing. She hummed and soon was singing, Mariah Carey's 'Hero.' It made her feel good. He even commented what a good voice she had. He hadn't realised.

"You could be a pro babe," he said. She knew he meant it, but she didn't want to sing in public, she was too shy and she liked to sing for the pleasure of it. It released something in her. She couldn't sing if she was sad. Lizzie pulled on her boots and prepared to meet the infamous Mrs Mac.

He took her to his local first. The Fox. It was a spit and sawdust type of place. She was amazed how he seemed to know everyone, including the barmaid, who looked her up and down, too intensely for Lizzie's liking.

'All right Tel,' various tough looking men greeted him and patted him on the arm. He introduced her to Gary 'Gal' Lennox and Baxter, no surname given, who Terry told her were mates from school and they went to the football together. She already knew that Terry was an avid Arsenal fan, he'd told her when they first met. It pleased her that he had missed the game yesterday to be with her, but they were ribbing him about 'being under the thumb' and he was taking it well.

Baxter was enormous, his gut spilling out over the waistband of his jogging trousers. It wasn't a pretty sight. Gary didn't match Terry in the looks department either, she decided. His teeth looked yellow and rotten. Weren't they in their twenties? At least Terry kept himself in shape.

He held her arm as the men chatted about football and the foul that Martin Keown had inflicted on Alan Shearer during the previous day's match. Lizzie switched off as she sipped her wine. Terry had downed his lager and was ready for another before she had half finished her glass.

"Get them in babe," he said handing her a twenty. As she bought the drinks at the bar, Tina the barmaid was quizzing her about Terry. Asking her how long they'd been seeing each other? Where had she met him? Lizzie decided she was nosey.

"What did you say?" Terry asked, scowling at Tina from a distance.

"I said we met a few weeks ago in Wanstead. Why is she so interested?" Lizzie wondered if she was one of Terry's 'conquests.

"Dunno," he said. "They're all like that round here, got nothing else to think about."

After another round of drinks, bought by Baxter, she felt giddy. She wasn't used to that much alcohol on an empty stomach. At home in Scotland her parents had sometimes given her a glass of wine with dinner. They thought it was part of growing up. She had a few ciders when she was at a party with her friends. This kind of drinking was alien to her. She wondered if she ought to ring her parents, then decided against it. They were expecting her home with her pride dented. They were in for a surprise.

After another pint, she persuaded Terry that it was time to go and see his mum. She didn't want to roll up at Mrs Mac's half cut and smelling like a brewery. After much back slapping with Gal and Brewster they left the pub under the watchful eye of Tina.

"It's Karaoke later," Terry told her with his arm around her waist. "Why don't you have a go babe? You could sing that song you were singing this morning. What was it, 'Hero' or something?"

Lizzie told him she wasn't sure she wanted to sing in front of 'that crowd.' He glared at her.

"What do you mean by that? Are my friends not good enough for little miss Posh?"

She didn't like the tone in his voice.

"I don't mean that Terry, I'm just shy. I don't want to show you up in front of your friends." This was the right answer. She sighed as he kissed her saying she wouldn't show him up. He would be proud of her.

"I'll think about it," promised Lizzie as they approached the door of the house in Drummond Street.

Mrs Mac opened the door in a plastic flowery apron. She was smaller than Lizzie imagined. No more than five feet two with hair scraped back into a bun and she had a fair bit of makeup on. Bright red lipstick, blue eye shadow. Lots of gold jewellery, maybe not real. She smiled at Lizzie and she relaxed straight away.

"Hello darling. Terence has told me all about you. Come on in sweetheart." She had a voice of deepest gravel from years of heavy smoking and a strong East London accent the same as Terry's. Mrs Mac ushered her into the small hallway and took her coat.

"We don't stand on ceremony here darling. Come in the kitchen and talk while I finish the dinner."

Terry went upstairs to change his clothes. The house was small, but cosy. She passed a lounge dining room that had been knocked through into the small galley kitchen at the back. Mrs Mac busied herself with the dinner, pouring the fat into the gravy from a large piece of roast beef, talking constantly as she did it.

"So you're from Scotland?" Lizzie told her about Edinburgh and her parents. She told her more than she'd intended to. Perhaps the wine had loosened her tongue.

"Adopted eh?" Mrs Mac thought about this. "Can't be easy love, but I bet they still love you to bits. They must be worried about you coming to the big city. Lizzie agreed, but told Mrs Mac she needed to stand on her own two feet. With the help of Terry of course. Mrs Mac smiled at the mention of her son.

"He's a good boy really. I would love him to settle down. It's all work, football and beer otherwise. I want some grandchildren while I can still enjoy them."

Lizzie winced. Was she hinting that she was the one? It was too soon to be thinking about children. Then she remembered they hadn't used protection. She could be pregnant right now. A panic came over her as she tried to smile at Mrs Mac.

"Don't worry darling. I can wait a little bit longer." She laughed, a deep chesty laugh. "Come and help me lay the table."

Lizzie put out the cutlery on the white cotton tablecloth. The lounge diner had more ornaments in it than she'd ever seen in her life. The place was spotless though and she wondered how many hours she took to dust them all. Terry had told her she was a cleaning freak. She asked her about her job, to turn the conversation away from children and settling down.

Alice McIntosh told her she had two cleaning jobs. She had cut back from three now she was pushing fifty six. She told Lizzie she had Terence later in life and hadn't thought she would ever conceive. He was her miracle and even after his father Phil, had left she had her 'Terence' to look after and keep her company. She told Lizzie that Phil had run off with a tart from Thailand.

"Maybe one of those Ladyboy brides. Stupid sod, she probably only wants him for his money, 'cause it can't be for anything else."

Terry came downstairs in a clean T-shirt and gave his mother a hug. He towered over the tiny woman and she looked up admiring her boy.

"Come on mum where's me roast?"

She dished up the dinner and poured out a glass of wine for both of them. "Liebfraumilch, my favourite. Terence always gets me a bottle don't you darling?"

Terry smiled at his mum. "I like to look after me old mum." They smiled at each other. Lizzie envied their closeness, but when his father abandoned them, they had nobody but each other.

They chatted as they ate their roast Topside. The meal was amazing and Lizzie praised her cooking.

"Can you cook darling?" Mrs M enquired.

"Not really, but I'm a quick learner. Perhaps you could teach me?" Lizzie didn't know where that had come from.

"I'm a traditional cook sweetheart. Nothing fancy. Shepherd's Pie, stew, all that kind of stuff. None of your fancy curries or chillies. Mind you Terence likes a take away don't you darlin'?" Terry nodded, his mouth full of Yorkshire pudding.

"Yeah mum you know I like my grub." Lizzie thought of the steak night and yearned for something more sophisticated. Her mum made a great risotto and her own pasta. Lizzie hadn't been truthful when she said she couldn't cook, but she wasn't great at roasts and pies.

Lizzie struggled to finish her dinner. The plate had been enormous. To follow Mrs Mac had produced an Apple Crumble and custard and Lizzie knew she couldn't refuse. It would be rude. She ate until she felt like she would burst. Mrs M's own portions were smaller she noticed. Terry polished off the lot with no trouble and asked for seconds after his first bowl of crumble. Alice gazed at her son.

"Love him. He still likes his mum's cooking.

"You're a hard act to follow mum," he said looking at Lizzie, "a very hard act."

12

Lizzie
30/12/1994

Lizzie put the finishing touches to her makeup. The hairdresser had just left and she wasn't sure about the cascade of curls she had created.

"You look fantastic sweetheart," reassured her 'soon to be' mother in law. Lizzie was unconvinced. Her hair felt almost crusty. Terry wouldn't be able to run his hands through it later. She was happy with the dress though and hoped Terry would like it. A classic design with a high front and an oval neckline. It scooped low at the back in a 'V,' showing off her delicate shoulder blades and the small of her back. Not the 'meringue' look that Mrs M had preferred. Instead, the bottom part of the dress flared out in an 'A-line,' meaning she could walk easier, thank God.

"Drink up your sherry sweetheart. It'll settle your nerves." Dressed in a purple two piece, she herself was puffing away on a cigarette and downed her own glass of sherry in one. It was a jacket and skirt with a glittery pink top underneath. A huge pink hat completed the outfit and given Mrs Mac was five feet two, she seemed to drown in fake Ostrich feathers. She was in her element though, organising Lizzie for her special day. Booking the hairdresser, helping her choose her dress and the flowers. She had done most of the organising in fact.

It wasn't Lizzie's dream wedding. Not that she had thought about it a great deal. She hadn't been one of those girls pouring over magazines and imagining herself walking up the aisle. It had just happened. She was eighteen. Too young perhaps, but she had been through so much over the previous year she felt as if she was at least thirty. Growing up fast, she had gone from being a pampered teenager to a young woman who had at least chosen to make her own way in the world.

Her parents were horrified when they heard about Terry and appalled that she wasn't coming home. She had found a flat and a job, though not the job they would have wanted for her, as an admin clerk in the council offices in Leyton. It was a job nonetheless, with a salary where she liked the people she worked with and it was only one stop on the tube from Leytonstone. With her wages and Terry's they had a comfortable standard of living.

Terry had moved in with her a few weeks after finding her the flat. He was strange though, he would always go to his mother's after a night out with the lads. He said he didn't want to disturb her, waking her up, smelling like a brewery. She knew he was thoughtful like that. She didn't like him when he drank too much. 'Volatile' was how she would describe him. Looking for an argument over anything. She preferred to see him in the morning when he was back to his normal self.

She wondered if this pattern would continue after the wedding. It might seem weird to Mrs M, if her married son kept coming home to sleep in his old room. Then again, knowing how she is, she wouldn't mind at all, thought Lizzie. She loved Terry's mum, she had a planet-sized heart, but she couldn't see any fault in her boy. Her 'Terence' was her prince and her life. Lizzie knew though that Mrs M approved of her daughter-in-law. Maybe that sealed the deal for Terry. Ever since the first time she had been to the house she had 'bonded' with his mother. Unlike her own parents.

They had turned up unannounced one Friday evening, a few weeks after she started work and Terry had moved in. She hadn't told them that piece of information. They thought she was living on her own, in a bedsit and they were not best pleased. Terry and Lizzie were in bed when the doorbell rang. Lizzie opened the door in a flimsy dressing gown shocking her parents to the core. They had hated Terry on sight. He sauntered towards them with his hand held out, dressed only in his boxer shorts.

"Pleased to meet you Mrs Forster," presenting himself as both cocky and arrogant. It got worse. They dressed whilst her parents sat in the living room. Then an almighty row ensued when they insisted that she come home with them. They accused Terry of ruining her education for God's sake. Lizzie was horrified. It was nothing to do with Terry.

She asked them to go. When they didn't, Terry stood up and looked almost menacing. They then left, her mother was crying and her father looked defeated. Afterwards she thought that maybe Terry could have acted more as a peacekeeper than a bouncer. In his eyes he was defending his girl, even it was from her own parents. She cried after they had left and he comforted her in the only way he knew, making love.

Lizzie tried to forget what had happened, but when they went for Sunday lunch to his mother's, she ended up confiding in Mrs M. She had been sympathetic, more so than her son, who by now had forgotten the episode and expected Lizzie to do the same. He had seen the way they looked at him, a mixture of disgust and shock that their daughter had chosen a working class builder for a boyfriend. It made him want her all the more.

Lizzie found it easier to leave them alone and stopped ringing. Terry got her a new mobile phone and when she asked for the old one, he said he'd 'chucked it.' They could have written, but they didn't, the contact stopped and Lizzie didn't want to make her peace with them. If they couldn't accept her new life, then they didn't deserve to be a part of it. She ignored the fact that they wanted the best for her. An education and 'a future' as her mother put it, not a dead end job in a council office. Perhaps it was about them, Lizzie thought. It's not about what I want. It's their expectations. What they would tell their friends. Terry was right they were snobs.

Mrs Mac was more philosophical. As she cleaned the kitchen sink, with a cigarette hanging out of her mouth, she told Lizzie it was hard being a parent.

"We don't always get it right sweetheart," she said, coughing into her hanky, not wanting Lizzie to lose contact with her mother and father, it wasn't natural. She couldn't imagine life without her Terence, or without Lizzie, who was now like a daughter to her.

Lizzie though, didn't waiver and decided, supported by Terry, not to invite them to the wedding. She had received some letters she knew her mother had written, from the envelope's spidery handwriting, but she binned them without opening them. She tried not to think about them. It was easier that way. They wouldn't have wanted to see her marrying Terry anyway, he wasn't a lawyer or a doctor and he wasn't Scottish.

She thought about the day Terry had proposed to her. It wasn't the most romantic of settings. They had been at the Romford Greyhound Stadium, Terry's favourite dog track when he fancied a flutter. After winning two hundred and thirty pounds on Brideshead, the greyhound, he had picked out because it was a small bitch with a cute face. The dog romped home and he said to Lizzie 'it was a sign.'

"Do you fancy being a bride babe?" He said, almost too casually.

"What do you mean Terry?" She asked, not daring to hope too much.

"Marry me Lizzie. You know we're a good team. I'll look after you. We don't need anyone else do we?"

She hesitated before saying yes. She didn't want to appear too keen.

"Yes, I would love to marry you Terry." He picked her up and swung her round. Gal and Baxter appeared at that moment, having been to the bar and they told them their news. Terry ordered champagne, even though he preferred lager. They toasted their happiness and both his mates were genuinely pleased for Terry & Lizzie.

They went out for a meal the following night for his 21st birthday. Mrs Mac wasn't surprised when he told her that Lizzie had agreed to be his wife. She knew she was smitten and couldn't have been more pleased. Lizzie was what he needed. She wouldn't always be around to look after her boy. Lizzie would do a sterling job. She had even managed under strict tuition to learn to cook a roast in true Mrs M style.

Lizzie wondered what Alice Mac would think if she knew about the baby. It still made her heart go cold when she thought about it. The abortion she'd had a few weeks into their relationship. She had wanted to keep the baby. Their baby.

Terry hadn't been well pleased. They were too young, he argued, they had their whole life ahead to think about children. He wanted to enjoy their time together, have some holidays and enjoy themselves before they had the responsibility of a child. Lizzie was unsure, but she let herself be swayed by Terry's persuasive arguments. He took her to the clinic in the Golf GTi he'd just bought. As the needle went into her arm and the anaesthetic took hold, tears were falling down her face as she thought about the child she was murdering. She had judged her own birth mother, for giving her away, but this was worse. This wasn't part of the plan.

When she woke up, it was all over and she felt a sense of loss, more poignant than she ever imagined. Terry picked her up and she looked at him with a sadness in her eyes he'd never seen before. It spooked him.

"Look babe, it wasn't a real baby, just some cells. We can have a baby when we're ready. I promise you."

She brushed her tears away and tried to forget about what she had done. They had told no one, especially Mrs M, who she knew would be devastated. It was their dirty secret. He always used protection now and she had gone to the doctors and asked them to fit a coil. Terry hated condoms, it spoiled his enjoyment, he told her.

When he proposed, her first thought was that maybe he would think about having a baby now. Her husband-to-be hadn't changed his mind though. Instead, he was planning their life together and had booked a honeymoon in Tenerife where it would still be warm. He told her not to mention it again. Not for a few years anyway.

Lizzie felt as though she had been cheated somehow. She imagined the baby, she had aborted, growing up. A little girl who would have been called Anna. This had to stop, or it would drive her mad, so she concentrated on Terry and making him happy. He was the future. They would have a family together one day, it would all be okay.

Terry's mother had arranged for a car to take them to the registry office in Waltham Forest. It wasn't the venue she'd wanted. A small church maybe, with an aisle to walk down. It wasn't to be. She couldn't have gone through with a church wedding after the abortion. It would feel like a sham. Also she wouldn't have felt right, marrying in church without her parents there. So she settled for the registry office ceremony and a reception in the rooms at the back of the Fox. They were laying on a disco and a spread of food. Mrs M had arranged it, made the food and Terry had paid for it. They had used most of her savings to buy the car and book the honeymoon.

Even though she had over two thousand pounds left, she wanted to hang on to in case of an emergency. Terry couldn't save, he was hopeless with money. Spending it like water, a 'cash is king' type of man who didn't like too much going in the bank for the tax man to find.

Terry wasn't ungenerous with his money, but she had to urge him to give her some to save for the future. They both wanted to buy a house, but the mortgage rates were sky high and the deposit would take some saving. Mrs Mac didn't own her house, she rented it from the same landlord she had for twenty five years. She urged them to buy their own home, saying she could have bought hers twice over by now.

The registry office was full when she arrived. Terry was already waiting in the front row, looking handsome in a blue suit and red tie. Scrubbed up well, his black hair gelled back, he didn't look as if he'd had a heavy last night, he was young enough to take it. Looking at Lizzie as she stood beside him, he smiled and the ceremony commenced.

Lizzie looked around at the congregation of people. They were all Terry's friends or family. His father hadn't made it from Thailand. He had sent them a cheque for five thousand as some kind of compensation. Terry had been angry, but he had still banked the cheque. Lizzie hoped it would go into their savings pot.

She hadn't invited friends from her previous life. No one had been to see her over the last year and she hadn't seen or heard from her friend Fiona for months. Fiona met Terry once, when they all went to a wine bar in Kensington. He hadn't much liked it, wanting to know why they didn't serve draught beer. Fiona had been pleasant enough and tried to make conversation, but it was obvious to Lizzie that she thought he was beneath her. The friends met once for coffee after that, but the friendship petered out. Lizzie was glad in a way, it was a reminder of her life in Edinburgh. She didn't want to think about her parents or what she had lost.

They had a limo to take them to the Fox. Her mother-in-law had decorated the huge room with enthusiasm. Flowers, ribbons and balloons, it was all somewhat overblown, but that was Mrs M and Lizzie loved her for trying. She had put up a huge banner, with 'Terence & Lizzie - 30th December 1994' printed on it. They had wanted to get married on New Year's Eve, but it was a Saturday and the pub was having a New Year bash, so they had to compromise. One of the many compromises Lizzie would make.

They welcomed their guests as they filled the room bringing gifts and cards and placing them on a large table set out for that purpose. No Wedding List had been sent out, so Lizzie had no idea what to expect. She hoped they wouldn't receive four toasters and three sets of knives. The 'Mother of the Groom' was in her element taking photos with a camera she had bought for the occasion. It had cost her a few quid, but it was cheaper than a photographer. Afterwards she presented them with an album, they had red eyes and looked too pale, as they gazed at the lens, but it was the thought that counted.

Lizzie looked startled in some of the photos and that was how she felt. It was all a bit surreal. The sherry had taken the edge off the anxiety of the proceedings, but she felt as though it was all a dream. The afternoon started off well enough with some fizz and the buffet, which was depleting fast. People were getting progressively more sloshed, including Terry who was already slurring his words.

Lizzie had an uneasy feeling in her stomach, wondering how it would turn out. The disco started at six and more guests arrived. Terry was staggering now and kept putting his arm around her and slobbering in her ear. She tried to laugh it off, but she worried that he would pass out.

He didn't, but he *did* pull his trousers down on the dance floor when the DJ found a copy of David Rose's 'The Stripper.' Lizzie was mortified. They had their first dance to 'Hero' and he stood on the train of her dress, ripping the hem. He didn't care, he was enjoying himself and everyone else seemed to find it funny. Some of his relatives were in a worse state than him. A fight broke out between Baxter and someone, who had come in from the street for a plate of free food. Terry joined in, but was soon pulled off the man who made a quick exit.

It was hardly the wedding of Lizzie's dreams in any sense, but the ever philosophical Mrs M said it wasn't a proper East End wedding without a fight. She said it was a great knees up, as all the older ones danced to the old cockney tunes the DJ had promised to play. Lizzie couldn't wait for it to end. She felt as if her smile would soon crack. It was licensed until midnight and by then everyone was well and truly mortal drunk. Terry had a glazed look now and he wasn't staggering, he was sitting, swaying.

They'd arranged for a taxi to pick them up, to take them to a hotel in the West End. They were due to fly from Gatwick the following afternoon. She had to pour Terry into the cab, who had become embarrassingly emotional as he kissed Gal and Baxter. Mrs Mac would clear the room up the next day and drop the gifts off at the flat.

By the time they arrived at the Crowne Plaza, Terry was asleep and snoring. She tried to wake him, but had to get the doorman to carry him in. He looked at Terry and couldn't hide his disdain, despite his professional manner. He looked at Lizzie with some pity.

The suite they'd booked was fabulous, but Lizzie couldn't enjoy it like this. She undressed Terry and realised he'd wet himself. This was their wedding night. It wasn't a good omen.

13

Terry
31/12/1994

I woke up and looked around. The clock said eleven. Where the fuck was I? Then I remembered. I was married. This was the hotel room. How did I get here? I vaguely remembered getting in to a cab. Where was Lizzie? She wasn't beside me. I crawled out of bed and my head felt like it contained seven dwarves with hammers. One in each hand. Oh my God, it must have been a good night.

Lizzie came out of the bathroom with a towel wrapped around her. She looked worse than me, what the fuck? Her eyes were red and she looked like she had been crying. What the bloody hell was wrong with her.

"Hello Mrs McIntosh." I thought I would try the Terry charm, despite my aching head and the urge to vomit. She looked through me. I pulled her towards me and she pulled away.

"You stink of piss and beer and fags, it's disgusting."

I slapped her across the face. How fucking dare she? We had the best wedding ever and this is how she thanks me. She fell to the floor and immediately I regretted hitting her so hard. I pulled her up.

"Babe I'm sorry I shouldn't have done that."

She cried and I felt like shit. I was still coming down from the coke I'd been sniffing in the toilets of the Fox and the hangover from hell.

I held her as she cried it out. Let her think that I hadn't known what I was doing. She lay in my arms and I stroked her. We talked about the wedding and I could see it hadn't been her thing. What was her thing? Everyone else had a good time. What was wrong with her?

She was trying to see it from my point of view, but she didn't understand about weddings in the East End. I tried to explain that to her and she softened a little.

A quick shower and breakfast, was called for. I needed to eat something, even if I couldn't keep it down. Her face was even redder now and I held a wet flannel to it, to stop it swelling. She looked so young in her robe, no makeup and I shouldn't have hit her.

"Look babe we're married now, it's all going to be great. We've got our honeymoon to look forward to. I promise I'll never do that again, okay."

She nodded. We kissed, as I held her face tenderly. I had some ground to makeup, but she needed to know who's boss.

14

Terry
30/12/1995

For our first anniversary. I wanted to make a special effort. I booked a table at the Steak House where we had our first meal and ordered some flowers to be delivered there. Who says men can't be romantic? Lizzie had said nothing about it. We've got an invite to a New Year's Party, but she hadn't mentioned our anniversary. Perhaps she has a surprise for me.

I don't think we've had a bad first year, though Lizzie might not agree. It didn't start well, the morning after the wedding wasn't great. I thought I had underestimated her and that she was tougher than she is. She didn't stand up to me enough though and she let me sweet talk her in the way only I can. A slap now and again doesn't hurt, does it?

She can make me angry. I love her to bits, but she doesn't understand how a man's mind works. When I get in from work, I need peace and quiet. Not her singing all over the place. The radio blaring drives me nuts. It all erupted the other night and I threw it at her. It missed though, thank fuck. We can laugh about it now. Well I can, 'cause I bought her a better one, so she shouldn't be moaning too much.

It's very frustrating when she's off in her own little world. I'm not old fashioned, but I do expect my dinner by seven, not bloody nine o'clock. Yes I know she goes to work every day, but she finishes at four thirty and it's one effing stop on the underground. If she got her act together she could make dinner in an hour. My mum always manages it. And she's got *two* jobs!

You have to set the boundaries in a marriage, I realise that now. Give them an inch and they'll take a mile. I don't like her going out with her mates from work, I know what they are like. I'm protecting her from herself, I know what men are like too. She is stunning when she is all dolled up and I don't want some other geezer trying his luck. She's mine. I don't think I am being unreasonable, it's different if I go out and it's just blokes talking football and shit. I won't go off with anyone, will I? I've got everything I need at home.

Marriage is all about compromise. I told her to invite the girls round when I am out. Have some wine, chick-flick films or whatever they do. I don't want her to be friendless. There's a few married women where she works, I don't mind them coming round. They can have a laugh and a few drinks, I haven't imprisoned her.

Anyway she needs to understand that I love her. I fucking adore her. I don't want anyone else to look at her, touch her, or talk to her. Well not in the chat-up way. Don't get me wrong I'm not one of those sexist men who think the woman is their property. She's her own person. It's the nineties for God's sake. I don't expect her to sit at home knitting. I gave her a hundred quid last week to go shopping in the West End. Told her to get some nice clothes, underwear, that sort of thing. I like her to look nice. She had a great day out. My mum went with her and I treated them to lunch. I'm a nice guy. Not perfect you understand, but my heart's in the right place.

Another bugbear is she keeps nagging me about kids. Ever since I got her pregnant in those first couple of weeks. Nothing wrong with my fishes by the looks of it, but kids would just spoil things. Noisy whinging brats, especially babies. I like my peace and quiet. Anyway a baby takes up all the mother's time. Everyone knows that.

I want her all to myself. While we're young enough to enjoy it. The sex is still good mind. I make an effort in that department. I don't want her looking anywhere else.

She nags me about my drinking too. That drives me nuts. I'm a builder, we get thirsty. Above all after work, a couple of jars with the boys. Doesn't hurt does it? It's not as if I overdo it during the week, I've got to get up at six for work. I like my Friday nights out with the boys though, it's normal, I'm twenty-two for God's sake. Most times I get home, she's asleep. I let her sleep, unless I'm feeling horny, then I just go for it.

She doesn't know about the 'charlie' though, even if she asks where all my money goes sometimes. Its forty quid a gram, but just on a Friday. It's not addictive you know, it's a buzz and it slows down the effects of the alcohol so you can drink more. I can get a bit lairy with it sometimes, but I've stopped fighting as much as I used to. Lucky for me I've never been caught. Wouldn't want a criminal record now would I?

So that's the pattern. Saturday morning's the boring food shop, but Lizzie won't learn to drive so I have to take her. I can go and put some bets on while she is in Sainsbury's and I often do. Every other week it's the Arsenal, but I didn't want to take the piss, so I've stopped going to the away matches mostly. Lizzie and I go out on Saturday nights, if I'm not too wasted. That's when the arguments start.

Anyway I don't want to think about that now. We're all right. We're fine, good together even. She's beautiful and she's my girl. I hope she likes my anniversary surprise, the meal and the flowers and that. I don't want her to think that I take her for granted.

15

Lizzie
A year or so later - 1997

Lizzie looked at herself in the mirror. She looked older, weary even. Her sparkle had gone. She needs to get it back. Applying makeup until she looks like herself, or at least the version of herself she prefers.

They're still in the same flat. It looks better now, the furniture has been upgraded. Shiny appliances in the kitchen. A nice bed and wardrobe, handmade from Antique Pine, but it's still the same flat. She'd hoped they would have moved by now. They have saved almost ten grand, including the five Terry's dad gave them. He has promised they can look in the New Year. Terry's not good at keeping his promises, Lizzie reflected with sadness.

He had promised not to hit her again after the first time in the hotel, but he had. Not that often, but he thought nothing of lashing out at her if he was angry. Terry was always sorry though, really sorry, even crying once, it broke her heart. He said he was scared he was turning into his old man and promised not to drink so much. Days later his selective memory couldn't remember saying it, which was the worst thing. Terry was possessive too, she knew that, but it meant he loved her, or so he said. He didn't want anyone else to look at her and accused her of chatting up the new barman in the Fox.

What a joke, he was a pleasant enough Australian guy, but she hadn't flirted with him, in fact she couldn't understand most of what he'd said. A combination of his accent and the rubbish on the Jukebox saw to that, but when they got home Terry went ballistic. His face was contorted with anger. She recognised the look now, before it got worse, but he drank Jack Daniels in the flat and that tipped him over. He pushed her down on the sofa and grabbed her by the throat. She convinced herself it was the alcohol. It wasn't as if he intended to strangle her. He seemed to realise what he was doing and pulled away, shortly before he passed out on the sofa.

When she told him the next day what he'd done, he didn't believe her at first, so she showed him the marks. He had the grace to look ashamed. He had a vague recollection of an argument about the barman, but couldn't remember attempting to throttle her. She told him he needed to get help, but Terry thought he just needed to stop drinking so much. For weeks after that he was on his best behaviour and even booked a weekend in Paris for them. While they were there he didn't drink too much and they had a great time seeing all the sights and feeling like young lovers again.

The Friday nights at the Fox stopped for a while too. They had nights in with a pizza instead. He was fine with a few beers, but Lizzie knew how much he could drink on a night out. She'd found some wraps in his jacket, more than once, so she knew he was using cocaine too. It wasn't the time to confront him about that now though, not now that things were getting better.

Lizzie planned a special meal at home for their anniversary. Steak the way he liked it and some baked potatoes. She bought him a funny card and told everyone it was their anniversary, feeling happier than she had for a while. Perhaps it took the incident with the barman to get him to come to his senses and appreciate her. He could be so loving when he wanted to be.

Lizzie didn't want him to stop seeing his friends, she liked the time on her own. Sometimes Maria or Shirley would come round from work and they would have a girl's night in, but she enjoyed being in the flat on her own too. She could put on a CD and sing to her hearts content. They just needed to have a happy medium, she decided.

16

Terry
A year later - 1998

My head feels like it is about to explode, as I look around the cell. I seem to be lying on a bunk bed on a blanket made of wiry dog hair. As my splitting head spins again, I lean over and vomit onto the stone floor. I'm not sure what's worse, the taste of the bile in my mouth, or the recollection of why I'm here. It's our third anniversary tomorrow and I'm in a Police Station cell feeling like I am going to die.

My memory's coming back and I can recall some of the night before. I'm trying to push the thoughts away, but they keep coming back to haunt me. Lizzie is screaming, as I pin her to the wall. I remember a knife. God I hope I didn't use it. I'll never get out of this place if I did. She was winding me up, that was it, saying I was controlling her and telling me she wanted to leave me. I couldn't let go of her, she was shouting, "you useless drunk."

It must have been a red mist moment and I pushed her up the wall. Where the knife came in, I'm not sure, it must have been to threaten her. I'd never cut her, not my beautiful Lizzie. Never in a million years. Those wanker neighbours downstairs must have called 999. I remember someone banging on the door and next thing some copper's got me round the throat. They must have knocked the door in after hearing her screaming like that.

I'm not blaming her for it, you understand. I shouldn't have threatened her, but what about 'for richer for poorer, in sickness and in health.' She has to stick by me, I can't live without her. It's all been going wrong lately, really wrong. They say you take it out on your nearest and dearest and it's true. It started in July when I was laid-off work. The company wasn't doing well enough and they lost a big contract for a leisure centre. Look, I haven't been out of work since I left school. I'm used to getting five or six hundred quid a week in my pocket. I'm used to getting up for work, having something to do all day and feeling useful. That all changed and not in a good way.

Lizzie still went to her office every day, but twelve grand a year won't float a sinking ship though will it? It's just enough to pay the rent, that's about it. I spent days looking around for another firm, but couldn't find any that were employing. Two of my mates were laid-off too, so we started to meet in the pub in the afternoon. It wasn't leisure you understand. It was networking. All the guys from the sites get in there after work for a couple. It's the only way to find out what's going on, who's hiring and that kind of info.

Lizzie didn't understand. She just saw I was using it as an excuse for me to go drinking and spend money we didn't have. Even my bloody mother joined in and agreed with her. Betrayed by my own mother, that hurt. What do they know anyway?

I dipped into the savings, without telling Lizzie, I didn't want to worry her and besides I'd put it back as soon as I got work. I told her I'd had wins on the horses and that kind of thing. She just changed like you wouldn't believe, accusing me of using coke, drinking, you name it. Okay I did use a bit, I needed a lift, unemployment is a depressing business, believe you me.

She found out about the money a week ago. There was four grand left out of the twelve we saved. I thought she'd faint, she went so white. She didn't speak to me for a week, a whole fucking week. I tried everything to sort it out. She wasn't having it. She didn't want to hear my reasoning that it was hard for me. It's tougher for a man you see, we're used to working and providing. Hunting and gathering, it's genetic I told her.

Anyway what was I saying? Oh yeah. Things were getting worse, we didn't talk, we didn't have sex, it was torture. I felt like she was punishing me. She certainly wasn't helping me with all her nagging. 'Stop drinking,' was the main one. I did for a while last year, but it wasn't long before I was back on it. It helps me relax, but I've got to admit I don't feel very relaxed right now.

Christmas was shit. I like Christmas, we normally go to mum's. This year was the same, but the atmosphere was different. I always buy some nice gifts for the two women in my life, but this year I couldn't. I didn't dare dip in the savings again and I couldn't even claim dole money because Lizzie was working. It was like she was holding the cards and holding them over me.

I promised her I wouldn't go out on Christmas Eve, but when Baxter came round I went for a couple that turned into ten. I couldn't say in front of my mates that the wife wouldn't let me out. They'd have thought I'd lost it and I couldn't have that.

I knew she would be upset when I got in and I was right. We had a screaming match, well I did. She was silent most of the time, apart from the bloody incessant crying. I threw a drink over her. That shut her up for a while. As you can imagine Christmas morning wasn't the best it could have been and by the time we got to mum's the ice hadn't thawed. Mum tried her best bless her. She did a lovely turkey as usual and tried to lighten the mood. I stayed on lemonade, but when mum brought out the port, I had a few. I was feeling better by then. Lizzie tried to make out everything was okay, she doesn't like upsetting mum, but she's not much of an actress.

Mum isn't stupid. She pulled me aside and asked me what was up. She knows I've got a temper, when I've had a few. I told her about the money problems and she offered to lend me a grand to tide me over. I cheered up at this point. If I had some money of my own, at least it might stop the arguing. I don't like taking it off the old dear, but as she said I might as well have it whilst she is alive rather than when she is gone.

Not that she is going anywhere. God Bless you mum, I said and slipped the cheque into my pocket. Lizzie was washing up, but she noticed the change in my mood when I went into the kitchen.

"Cheer up babe, I'll get it all sorted. I promise you. Don't give up on me." I kissed her gently, but she didn't return it. Her mouth felt cold.

To cut a long story short, she found out about the money. She knew I'd cashed it through a friend's account. I don't know how, maybe going through my phone, the snidey cow. I stormed out the house and went to the pub. Quite a few Jack D's and numerous lines of coke later I was still fuming. The boys tried to calm me down. I hate being checked up on. There has to be trust in a relationship I think. She should have let me sort myself out. My next mistake was fucking Tina on the pool table. I hadn't been there for ages, it wasn't a regular thing. A man likes to feel wanted though and she always had a soft spot for me.

Well that would've been bad enough, but my biggest mistake was telling Lizzie about it when I got in. About how hot for it Tina had been and how much better she was than Lizzie at shagging.

I said it to hurt her, but that's when she said she was leaving me, so I picked up the knife to make her stay. I didn't want to live without her, ever, I'd rather kill her than let her leave. Did I really say that? Of course I didn't mean that either, but I couldn't let her go.

The door of my cell rattled and a Policeman came in to take me in for questioning. He cautioned me and asked if I wanted a brief. I told him I did and he rang the solicitor my dad had used a few times, when in a spot of bother. He took two hours to get to the station so I had time to think about what I would say. He told me to say 'no comment' to any questions they asked. They didn't seem to have a lot to go on anyway, it looked like Lizzie hadn't given a statement. They said they were going back to see her later on.

Bailed to return to the Police Station the following week, I was advised to stay away from Lizzie. Not a fucking chance of that I thought, as I made my way back to the flat. I didn't have a key, so I rang the bell. She opened it, eyes wide when she saw it was me. I'm so sorry, I started. It was easy to cry, I felt so sorry for myself. She looked at me with a mixture of love and hate. She was crying too.

"I'm pregnant," she blurted out. Those two words changed everything. She wouldn't leave me now, she couldn't, could she?

"I'll change. We can be a family. I'll find work babe, anything."

She looked at me and smiled. A hopeful smile.

17

Lizzie
A year later - 1999

Lizzie realised that she had stopped singing. She couldn't remember when she had last sung anything, even to sing with the radio. It was as if her voice had gone, along with her identity and her mojo. How did being depressed differ from being sad? She wondered this as she swallowed one of the tablets the doctor had given her. She remembered that Mrs Mac, who she now called mum, had called them 'mummy's little helpers' and had then realised what she had said and changed the subject.

Lizzie wasn't a mummy. She should have been a mummy in August, but it wasn't to be. A miscarriage in April meant she had the traumatic and heartbreaking experience of giving birth to a dead baby boy. She had cried. Terry had cried. Mrs Mac could barely hold it together.

Lizzie and Terry had tried to sort things out when she found out she was pregnant. He had promised to change and he did for a while. He found work with another building company, albeit not as well paid, and the nights out stopped. She tried to forget the things he'd said about Tina the barmaid. He back pedalled and said that he had lied to hurt her, he'd never touch Tina, she wasn't even his type. She knew he was lying.

Lizzie had given him another chance, for the sake of the new life growing inside her. They knew it would be a boy, the scan had shown his genitals and Terry had laughed, saying he would be well endowed like his dad. They called him Jack. It was a name they both liked. A straightforward boy's name.

Lizzie spent hours imagining what he would be like, would he have his dad's looks and be a heartbreaker. Those blue eyes and dark hair. Or would he look more like her, but she didn't care, she wanted to hold him in her arms. Terry would change when he became a dad, wouldn't he? They would spend weekends taking Jack to the Park and to the seaside. It would give Terry a focus, he was already planning to take him to the Arsenal. He has seen the tiny Babygros in the fan's shop and planned to buy his first outfit.

Lizzie felt the first pains when she was in the shower. She had banned Terry from having sex in case it hurt the baby. It was an old wives tale, but she didn't want to take any chances. He wasn't happy about that. They had argued earlier in the day when he woke up with his 'morning glory' and suggested anal sex instead. Lizzie was appalled. Had she not been pregnant he would have given her a slap, she was sure.

The Police woman from the Domestic Violence Unit, who came round after she'd dropped the charges against him, warned her that pregnant women were more vulnerable. She couldn't believe that, what kind of man assaults a woman, pregnant with his child. Not Terry, he wasn't that kind of man. They gave her all kinds of leaflets, should she need help. The Police Officer told her that violent men, often couldn't or wouldn't change. It was a pattern. Lizzie didn't relent though, she didn't want to put Terry in prison.

When she refused to have sex with him, his face contorted in that old familiar way and she noticed his eyes get closer together. She hadn't seen him like this for a long time. He thought sex was his right. She was his wife. He had spoken to all his mates and their fathers, no one knew anything about sex affecting the baby. She looked at him wondering where this was going. As he went to grab her, to force himself inside her, she rolled over and fell out of bed on to her stomach. It was an hour later that she realised she was losing the baby.

Now she was on the happy pills and she'd stopped going to work. She couldn't face the sympathetic glances of her friends and colleagues. No one knew the truth, the real truth. Only she and Terry knew. She blamed herself for upsetting him. She blamed him for wanting sex. It didn't matter now, Jack was no more. She felt as if she was in a pit of despair.

Terry told her to pull herself together. She wondered if she pulled herself together well enough, if she'd have the strength to leave him. She saw beyond the macho façade that was Terry. He had cried too. She felt trapped. There was no way out. She had made her bed and now she must lie in it.

18

Terry
30/12/1999

I remember when I was a kid, the things you looked forward to were always shit. The best times were the unplanned ones, the parties after the pub, the day out when mum and dad decided on the spur of the moment to go to Southend. You know the thing I mean. It's the same with this millennium thing. The Year 2000. We're supposed to see the start of something big. It's all going to be different, it's the year 2000, it must be Space age, or something like that.

New Year's Eve's always a knees up and I've had some good and bad ones in my time. All that hugging and shaking hands. Let old acquaintances be forgot and start afresh. There are more punch ups on New Year's Eve than any other night I reckon.

This hasn't been a good year. I didn't party like it was 1999, despite what Prince might say. I tried my best last New Year's Eve, but Lizzie with her face like a pan of piss was enough to put anyone off. She seemed to forget we had both lost Jack, our little fella. If that clumsy cow had been more careful, he might be here now. She couldn't get over it, crying all the time.

Thank God for work. I had a contract in Brighton, so stayed away four nights a week, give us both a break from each other. Mind you, when I would rock up on a Friday she never seemed all that pleased to see me. At least I didn't have to worry about her seeing anyone else, given the state of her, no one would look twice.

I wondered how it would all pan out. I don't think that she would have snapped out of it, if it hadn't been for two things. One of them was my idea. I bought her a little dog. A Shih Tzu or something like that. A bloke at work was selling some puppies, so I thought I would get her one. She would have to look after it, get out the house and take it for walks and stuff. She would have something to concentrate on, other than herself. I thought it was a terrific idea. I surprised her and one Friday night in February took it home and put it under my coat. It was an ugly little thing, but that's not for me to say.

I opened the door with the dog in my coat. She was lying on the sofa as usual, staring at the TV screen. She was on those 'happy' tablets, so she looked out of it most of the time. I tried not to think about what had happened to my sexy girl. She sat up as I came in and rubbed her eyes. She must have been sleeping, it was what she did best at the time. Then she saw the movement in my coat.

"Terry, I wasn't expecting you this early."

She looked like a stag in the headlights. You know, startled.

"I was going to do a casserole for dinner, I've got the stuff in already."

I pulled out the dog. It was tiny and fitted into my hand. She squealed and actually looked happy, for the first time in a long time. She cradled the little dog in her arms. It licked her and she was infatuated.

That was the best weekend for a long time, even though I couldn't stand the thing, it yapped and fussed. She called it Frankie. It was Frankie this and Frankie that, but we went out and she bought some bits for it. It looked fucking stupid on its little lead. I like a real dog, like a German Shepherd or something. Lizzie was happy with Frankie. We had sex for the first time in ages that weekend. She kept thanking me for getting the dog. It lay on our bed, like it owned the place. Anyway it would keep her company while I was away.

The other thing was mum. Old Alice Macintosh wasn't well. She had a hacking cough that was getting worse, probably due to the 'forty a day' smoking habit she had since she was fifteen. I had stopped, it wasn't easy, but it saved me a fortune. Mum couldn't stop, but I worried about the cough and so did Lizzie. She was back and forth to the doctors having tests and more tests. I know she had an inkling, but no one wanted to say anything outright. You don't do you? The doctors confirmed that it was cancer and it had already spread to her lungs and liver.

She is a scrapper though my old mum. When she started the chemo, I never heard her complain about it. She even got a wig when her hair fell out. Lizzie and mum went up West to a special shop. That's what I mean when I say things changed. Lizzie stopped feeling sorry for herself and supported mum. It was harder for me, working away, but I needed to be the breadwinner. Lizzie had packed up her job and mine was the only wage. I couldn't splash as much on beer, or coke, or anything else I fancied now. I paid the rent and bills and there was damn all left over.

Mum is a stubborn old girl and she did her best to get over it all, bless her. I saw her every Sunday, but Lizzie would go over now and cook the dinner. Mum ate like a bird and I could see her wasting away. In September she went to the hospice. Lizzie went every day until she took her last breath on bonfire night.

Lizzie summoned me back from Brighton when the doctors had said she might not last the night. I was lucky to get back in time. I held her hand and she slipped away. Not before telling me to shape up and stop acting like my old man. That upset me. Mum had more insight than she let on. Nothing much got past her.

"You have a good girl there Terence," she spluttered. "Don't screw up." I looked at mum's face. Her eyes were sunken, her skin like paper. It was spooky. She didn't look like mum anymore. I wanted out of there, quick. I didn't want to hear her telling me to look after Lizzie, she should tell Lizzie to look after me.

"Don't leave me mum," I said. Where did that come from, I wondered? I'm supposed to be the hard man. Swallowing back tears, I remembered how many years we'd been on our own. She should have had a better son. It was too late now. Mum's eyes flickered as she passed like she was in a deep, deep sleep. Lizzie had come back in the room by then. We were both in tears. Somehow mum had held it together. She was the only family either of us knew. If I had any brakes, then mum was the brakes. What would happen now? It didn't bear thinking about.

The funeral took the last of our savings because I wanted mum to have a good send off. She had wanted a funeral, none of that 'quick few words and disappear through the curtains to music' crematorium stuff for her. Her coffin, decorated with M U M in flowers and the horse driven carriage was her last request. I remember little after the funeral itself. I couldn't do a speech or anything, I was too upset and left that to the vicar. He spoke of her kindness, hard work, common sense and someone who was always there for her friends and family for help and advice. He was right. She was a diamond my mum.

The wake was held in the same room in the Fox where Lizzie and I had our wedding reception. We had ordered in some catering, well Lizzie had and decided not to have a free bar. We couldn't afford to foot the bill for drinks, not the way my mates drink. Lizzie had made a CD recording of all mum's favourite songs, the old East End knees up numbers, and some of her favourites from the sixties. She liked Tamla Motown my mum, she would get Lizzie to sing all her favourites, 'Dancing in the street,' 'Baby love,' anything from that era. It was comforting to hear the tunes, but upsetting as well if you know what I mean.

I knew I'd get drunk. I had to get drunk, had to forget what was going on, that I'd never see my mum again. I'm an orphan. Well I might as well be, my dad hadn't even returned the phone call I'd made to him, to tell him about the funeral. He must have thought I wanted a contribution. Maybe I did. Selfish bastard. Mum is worth ten of that bloody thing he calls his wife. I decided there and then I would never speak to him again.

A couple of lagers, then I moved onto the Jack Daniels. I knew Lizzie would monitor my consumption, so I kept a half bottle in my pocket I could nip into the 'Gents' and have a crafty swig.

So many people were approaching me to pay their respects, it was doing my head in. Lizzie was doing the rounds, with some of mum's friends, with that stupid little dog in her arms. She had even found a coat for it in black. It was out of order.

The anger was building up inside me as the day went on. Mum was only sixty-three for God's sake. She should have had years ahead of her. What would I do without her? She adored me, despite my faults. No one will ever do that again. Lizzie wasn't the adoring girl I'd first met. I knew she was sick of me, sick of my behaviour towards her, but look at what I'd had to put up with, her moods and her depression.

I continued with the JD until my throat burned and then some. It helped, it helped a lot, but I wasn't maudlin. Mum loved that word, she accused me of it many a time when I had drunk too much. Maudlin and angry, that's what she said the drink turned me into. She always said it wasn't me, it was the drink, it gets some people like that. Mum loved a sherry, or her precious Liebfraumich. Disgusting stuff, tasted like perfume. I laughed to myself as Lizzie approached me, Frankie yapping. I could tell it didn't like me that precious little bastard.

"What are you laughing at Terry," she asked with that snobby look I hated. She was in a black dress. It had a low front. Too low; showing her tits. It wasn't decent. It was mum's wake for God's sake. I scowled at her and her stupid dog. I should have got her a new handbag instead, I realise that now. She spent more time fussing round that little shit than she did on me.

"I've been thinking Terry," Lizzie went on, "perhaps I should contact mum and dad? It's been so long and since seeing mum and we never know how long we've got do we?" She was still looking at me in that way. The anger was building now.

"Oh I see how it is. I'd forgotten you still had *your* parents. It's all right for you isn't it princess?" I snarled the words at her. How fucking dare she mention them now. I couldn't believe what I was hearing.

"'Where were they when we needed them eh? It was *my* mum who comforted you when Jack died. Just fucking remember that?" The dog was whimpering now. It wasn't as stupid as it looked, unlike its owner.

Lizzie was trying not to cry and stammering, something she had started to do lately.

"I, I, I thought you would be pleased."

"Pleased? Oh yeah, I'm fucking delighted." I left her standing there and headed for the lavatories. Lucky Baxter had thought of everything and he offered me a line of the best coke he'd been able to get. As I inhaled the drug, it took its effect and I felt strong again. Powerful and able to take on the world, even without my precious mum.

19

Lizzie

It wasn't ever going to get better. She knew that now. She was aware and had been for some time she had married a monster. A monster with a winning smile and the face of an angel. Apart from when it contorted into 'that face,' the one she knew would hurt her and would continue to hurt her until he felt better about himself.

She had held it together over the last few months for the sake of Mrs Mac. The tiny woman with the big heart who saw the best in everyone, especially her own child. As her morphine intake had increased, she had become more lucid when it came to her 'Terence'. She told Lizzie things about him, she would never have disclosed, if she hadn't been dying and under the influence of the medication.

Mrs M told her of Terence's cruelty and the things he had done as a child, but blamed his father saying he was a 'chip off the old block.' She told Lizzie how he had spoiled any relationship she tried to start, by his behaviour. He didn't want a stepfather and he made that clear. Chilling stuff, like the time he smeared her makeup all over her face, to stop her going out, telling her she was an old hag and no one would want her anyway.

Even with her death looming, Mrs M tried to defend him. It was her fault. She had spoilt her son and she shouldn't have let him get his own way so often as a young child. Lizzie listened and held her hand, not saying much.

Mrs Mac's tongue loosened further with the morphine and she talked and talked, remembering things a mother shouldn't have to remember. She spoke of a mother's love. It allowed her to love her boy, despite knowing what he was. He had seen a child psychologist when he was eleven. The school arranged it. She read the report then burnt it. Told herself it was nonsense.

The woman thought her Terry was a bloody psychopath or sociopath, or something like that. How could you say that about an eleven year old boy? He was a child for God's sake, a mixed up child. She knew he liked to hurt people and about the football violence. They all do that though, don't they? It gets it out of their system. Yes he could be cruel, but he had a loving side to him too. He just needed to be pointed in the right direction.

Lizzie was disturbed by what Mrs Mac was saying. More than disturbed, frightened in the depth of her stomach. She had always feared the violence she knew Terry was capable of, but in her naivety had believed it was all about her. Her shortcomings, her inability to manage his moods and make things right. He was her first love. No, he was her only experience of love.

She knew now in her heart that Terry was incapable of love. He could give the impression of someone who could love and have feelings, but the passion he had shown to her in the beginning, was possession. She remembered the second time they had made love. No, not made love, had sex. He had forced himself on her. Raped her even. She hadn't wanted him, it was all about his needs, his desires. Even the abortion hadn't affected him. He could cut off from the emotions, the normal human emotions.

She tried not to think about their baby. Jack, the little boy who never stood a chance. If she hadn't been trying to get away from her husband, Jack would be alive now.

A toddler, laughing and playing. She was in a rut of despair as the realisation hit home.

She looked at her husband as he laughed and joked with his friends. They had just buried his mother. His face was red with the booze already and it was mid-afternoon. She could see into the future. See their lives together as his anger became harder and harder to manage. He would kill her, of that she was sure. Either emotionally or physically, it didn't much matter which.

Terry had already destroyed a part of her, during their time together. She had no confidence left and no more self-esteem either. She looked in the mirror and saw a stranger. A sad empty shell of a woman stared back. She should have been in the prime of her life. Instead, she couldn't even see any hope.

Lizzie had to get away from him, it was the only way. To start again, to rebuild herself. She had to do it, to survive. She wondered if she had the strength to go through with it. More than once he'd told her that if she left him he would hunt her down and find her wherever she was. If he couldn't have her, no one would have her. That sounded like an old cliché, but in his case it was true. Maybe she could never be free of him.

She saw him sneering at her, looking down at little Frankie who was already whimpering with fear. Dogs know, she thought. He'd never been overtly cruel to the dog, not in her presence anyway, but she knew something had happened when she was out. The little dog was now terrified of Terry. She felt sick.

It had taken the sad death of her mother-in-law to make her come to her senses. Terry would never change, that was the frightening thing. He was the same cruel person he had been as a boy, just older not wiser, but more dangerous and a lot more cunning. He thought he was invincible.

She dreaded the night that would follow the day. This awful day. She knew he was back on the coke. That and the Jack Daniels he had in his pocket. When the two substances combine, they release the man that hides inside the shell. She wondered if she should go now, while she still could, but where? She had no money, he had seen to that. The last of their paltry savings had gone on Mrs M's send off. She had less than a pound in her purse. Where could she go with eighty eight pence? She couldn't even get on a bus for that.

Lizzie was trapped, until she could squirrel away enough money to make her escape. She would need to be careful, he would read her phone messages and he always seemed to know her innermost thoughts.

He mustn't suspect, if he even has a suspicion she's leaving, it could be fatal.

20

Terry

I should know by now when I've had enough. I should have that button that other people seem to have, to stop drinking and go and sleep it off. Maybe getting lairy or feeling like you are in someone else's body. I often get to that stage where I think I am watching a movie. The movie is me, whatever I am doing is happening to someone else and I am just watching. It's like an out of body thing. I like it in a way. I tried LSD once, but all that tripping sent me mad. This way I am still in control. Well almost in control. Just no inhibitions if you get my meaning.

I told Lizzie to get rid of the crowd. It was over now. I couldn't stand there being nice to people any more, some who didn't know mum droning on about her. I didn't want to lose it, but I was coming close. When Baxter beckoned me to the toilets, for another line or two, I knew I shouldn't. What the hell, you only live once, eh mum?

By the time I came out, there were a few stragglers left. They had demolished the food, greedy bastards. It was over. Lizzie held my arm as we left to walk home. I could see people looking at me in a strange way. I know what you're thinking, coke makes you paranoid, but seriously they were looking at me as if I was scum. Out the corner of my eye I could see them whispering and pointing. Lizzie tried to make light of it, but they were proper pissing me off. If I had been at Arsenal, I'd have been tooled up. No fucking problem. But not here, not now.

I took a deep breath as we got outside. It was raining I seem to remember. That bastard dog was whining. He didn't like the wet. Didn't like it when I held his little head under the tap either, I seem to remember.

Lizzie was pulling me up the stairs. My feet felt like lead, I was coming down fast from the last few lines and it wasn't a good feeling. I felt for my keys, but Lizzie was already opening the flat door. I fell inside, I think. She was mumbling something about making some food. That would make me feel better, I remembered I had eaten nothing all day.

I lay down on the sofa, the room was spinning now. Lizzie was busying herself in the kitchen. She shouted out that she would make a roast, in honour of Mrs Mac. The thought turned my stomach. I was past food by that stage.

The next thing I remember is waking up to the smell of cooking. That horrible fatty smell, combined with cabbage or some other vegetable. It smelt vile. My mouth felt like sand, I could feel the spittle in the corner gluing my lips together. I was finding it difficult to speak. I looked at the clock. It was nearly ten. The woman was mad. I struggled to get on my feet and headed to the kitchen. Lizzie was spooning fat over the roast potatoes, wearing an apron. What happened after that was more of a blur, but I remember feeling a surge of rage that seemed to start in my feet, moving slowly up my body. Everything was in slow-motion, as if I was swimming in treacle.

21

Lizzie

T erry looked at Lizzie with hate in his eyes. His eyes reddened by the drink and drugs seemed almost demonic. He was trying to talk, but spitting at the same time. Lizzie felt the rage emanating from his every pore. It had been a long time coming, she thought, almost calmly. It had all been leading up to this moment, from early in the day. Or her life come to that. She was past fear. The horrible feeling of anxiety in her stomach had turned to stone. She felt nothing.

She watched him pick up Frankie from his basket in the corner of the room. Her limbs were incapable of movement. She felt as if she had been given an anaesthetic and it was taking effect. She opened her mouth to scream, but no sound came out. Her instincts to protect Frankie kicked in and she tried to grab him from Terry who was now making a sound that resembled a growl. It wasn't coming from Frankie, whose little body was rigid with fear as Terry held him around the throat with one hand. The other hand pushed her back, on to the ground. She heard him going to the door and tried to get up.

Lizzie wasn't quick enough to save him, but she was quick enough to see Terry throw Frankie down the stairs. She *was* in time to hear the thud as his small body hit the bottom of the stairs and onto the landing. She heard his little skull crack as it hit the wooden stairs. He missed the carpet weaving up the middle, and landed squarely on the wood. There was no sound from him at all. Not a whimper. She knew he was dead.

Terry was snarling now, looking like Satan himself. His red eyes glowing in the light of the hallway. He pulled her back inside and pushed her toward the kitchen. She wondered how he would kill her. Would he go for the knife drawer? Would it be quick? He lost his footing and she tried to get past him. He regained his balance and pushed her with all his strength until she was back lying on the cold floor once more.

Her life didn't flash in front of her, she just lay there immobile now as he poured the pan of hot fat and potatoes over her. She felt the burning on her face and her arms, yet the scream she could hear wasn't coming from her mouth, it was inside her head. He kicked her as she lay on the ground, anywhere and anyhow he could. She imagined him on match day, laying in to one of the opponent's supporters, instead of his wife. She must have blacked out, either with the pain or the fear, or both.

When the Police arrived, they recognised the address from previous call-outs. The downstairs tenant was hysterical, holding a small creature in her arms that looked like a skinned rabbit. It was her neighbour's dog as it turned out. It was dead and they wondered about the fate of his wife upstairs. Was he still in the property? They were used to this type of work, but neither Officer was prepared for the sight of Mrs McIntosh lying on the kitchen floor covered in fat and potato. Her pretty face swollen beyond recognition and they wondered if she was still alive.

Terry turned around and smiled at them. They soon realised he was totally insane or off his face on something. His trousers were around his ankles, his penis in his hand and he was urinating over his motionless wife. Fortunately for the Officers, because his trousers were restricting his movements, they could cuff him easily.

"Jesus Christ," said one of them. He had seen some sights in his time, but this was one of the worst. The neighbour had called an ambulance and it was at the door as they were putting him into the car. The young WPC who was with them, stayed with Elizabeth. Her pulse was faint, but they had realised that at least she was still alive. As Rachel Thomas held her hand she wondered what kind of world it was where a man could do this to a woman. His wife, the love of his life. Tears fell on her cheeks and she lost any innocence that still remained after eighteen months in the Domestic Violence Unit.

22

Suzanne Taylor

Suzanne Taylor had been a Probation Officer for more years than she cared to remember. She had completed her training in the year Charles married Diana and she wondered not for the first time why she was still doing the job. A staunch feminist, she'd seen male violence over the years that confirmed that men thought they ruled the world. Even if they didn't, most wanted to at least rule in their own homes.

She had seen sights that had turned her stomach and made her question humanity. She knew the reasons that drove these men to act in the way they did. The theoretical knowledge that they need to exert power and control. Taking it any way they could, emotionally, financially, sexually and violently.

Knowledge and training didn't make the job any easier though and she knew that if she stopped feeling disgust and outrage, she would leave the job for ever. She hadn't yet lost the conviction that she could make a difference. Or at least offer the women protection and safety and try to persuade them to use the services provided. The refuges were full of victims, their children and their lives destroyed by the men they professed to love.

It was Sue's job to work with the perpetrators of such violence. To change their behaviour and get them to see the error of their ways. It was a thankless task. The domestic violence programmes in her view only scratched the surface. The dangerous ones, like Terry McIntosh would never change, it was their nature, to their core. She had seen the Psychological reports written when Terry first appeared at Court. His lawyer had thought he was doing him a favour, but the evidence put forward about his psychological state was damning.

The Psychopathy test was likely to be the only one that Terry would pass with flying colours. He had no regard for anyone but himself and with no remorse, apart from how his terrible crimes had impacted on his own freedom.

He could try and pretend and was charming when he wanted to be, but he hadn't fooled the professionals. They had seen the reports from when he was a child. Terry was a dangerous man and his wife was lucky to be alive. If the neighbours hadn't acted when they did, Lizzie would now be dead or a vegetable at least. She had made a remarkable recovery, however Sue wondered if the psychological scars had healed too.

Terry had been in custody now for three years. Sue had written his pre-sentence report for the Court and recommended that he receive a sentence for Public protection. An indeterminate sentence, meaning he would be released when it was safe to do so. Unfortunately the judge hadn't agreed with her assessment and that still bothered her to this day.

His lawyer told the court of the death of his mother, his alcohol and drug problem, and persuaded the Judge to sentence Terry to eight years in prison. He would be out for good in a year. He had applied for temporary home leave in the meantime, telling the authorities he was a changed man. The model prisoner. Completing all the courses required of him. Telling the Parole Board of his genuine remorse and shame. It had been a good performance.

Sue knew it was an act. He still made the hairs on the back of her neck stand up when she interviewed him in prison.

He was allowed home leave to go to a hostel in central London. The purpose had been to test him in the community and see if the courses he had undertaken had made him less of a risk. He would be given a weekend of freedom with some curfews, keeping him in the hostel from eleven pm to nine am. The time in between was his own, but he would be tested for alcohol and drugs during his time there. Sue prayed he would screw up and go to the pub, or take some cocaine. Anything, as long as it delayed his release date and keep him away from Lizzie.

There was the surprise. She had stuck by him. Despite everything that had happened, his wife had visited him once a month and told the Parole Board she wanted him home. Sue had initially been gobsmacked. The woman was intelligent and came from a good Edinburgh home. She had experienced an attack that could have killed her, yet she was willing to give him another chance. Sue would never understand these women. She had spoken to the Domestic Violence Unit, who had confirmed they had visited Lizzie frequently and had issued her with an 'Osman warning.'

Osman warnings are official documents introduced after a case where the victim had gone back to the perpetrator and been killed. The police were found to be negligent in their duty to protect Mr Osman. Now they're used as warnings to persons at risk of harm from particular individuals and that further contact with them is at their own risk.

It meant that if Lizzie stayed with Terry she could expect further violence and the Police had done their best to dissuade her. It was their 'get out of jail' card absolving them of any responsibility, but it's a warning not given out lightly. Lizzie had signed the documents, almost serenely, nodding to say she understood.

It got worse. She asked for Terry to go back to their flat, if the home leave went well and he was freed by the Parole Board, on his release date. Sue knew that she couldn't keep them apart unless Lizzie wanted it that way. Victim liaison had got nowhere with her, she hadn't wanted to engage. She could have moved away or changed her name. There were protective measures available in this type of case.

Sue knocked on the door of the house. She had written to Lizzie saying she wanted to visit her at home and look at the situation of Terry's move back home in December. His first weekend release was in eight weeks' time, maybe she would want to see how it goes before making a final decision. If he messed up she would see he hadn't changed at all.

Lizzie opened the door and led Sue up the stairs to the flat. It was very quiet. Lizzie smiled as she let her in. It was immaculate, it almost looked like a show home, hardly lived in at all. The furniture was all cream, as were the carpets and walls. A few pictures and cushions strategically placed and that was it. She looked at Lizzie. The scars on her face had faded, with treatment she guessed. Her long dark hair hung down her back, shiny and straight. She was expertly made-up and at first glance you couldn't notice the burns.

Lizzie offered Sue a drink and went into the kitchen to make coffee. Sue followed her into the galley kitchen, recognising it from the pictures she had seen in the Crown's documents. How could she stand to be in here, knowing what had taken place? She wanted to ask her, but didn't know how to put it. She had to be sensitive to the woman whatever she felt about her situation.

Lizzie told Sue the reasons she wanted Terry home. She told Sue she wasn't deluded, or stupid. He had changed. It had all got too much for him, his mother's death, the drinking and the cocaine. She also told Sue she had completed a degree in Psychology during the time Terry had been in custody. This gave her an understanding of his upbringing and the pain of his father's rejection. She could help him now, help him become the person he was destined to be. A husband who would respect her and understand that he had a second chance.

Sue brought Lizzie back to reality when she talked about the diagnosis of anti-social personality disorder, with possible psychopathic traits. Lizzie nodded, but she then went on to say he was on anti-psychotic medication in the prison. It was working. Lots of people suffered from these disorders and led normal lives. Lizzie talked at length, about how people believe that all psychopaths are killers, or criminals at the very least.

That wasn't true, Lizzie tried to assure Sue, who had heard it all before from other professionals. Most go on to live productive lives, as long as they take their medication. It stabilises their moods. Lizzie explained that Terry's moods altered with alcohol and drugs. He had in her view 'self-medicated,' but with the wrong drugs. He knew something wasn't right, but it was the worst thing he could have done.

Sue was surprised at the capable young woman sitting next to her on the sofa. This wasn't what she expected at all. Lizzie didn't have the persona of a 'victim,' she seemed in control of the situation and her own life. She believed in Terry and told Sue, "I know him better than anyone else in the world."

Sue asked Lizzie about their married life. The previous violence, the call-outs by the Police, the reluctance to prosecute. How could she protect herself if things didn't work out? Lizzie smiled again. She would accept a panic button installed by the Police and the authorities could visit anytime they wanted. Also, if she thought for one minute that Terry was slipping back to his old ways, she would be gone.

"But it won't happen," she said with sincerity. "I know it looks like I'm crazy, but believe me I'm no fool."

Sue left the flat feeling confused and off kilter. She couldn't get the measure of Lizzie Macintosh at all. It sounded so plausible, but there was something that just didn't ring true. It was a feeling she couldn't shrug off. She knew she wasn't wrong about Terry. Her assessment skills had sharpened over the years and she knew Lizzie might have convinced some people, but not her. She hoped for Lizzie's sake she was wrong.

23

Terry

I'm free. Fucking hell I'm free. Okay only for a weekend, but it feels amazing. As I walked away from the prison gates with a small bag on my shoulder I was smiling with a grin wider than a Cheshire cat. I don't care about the shithole hostel. I'm out of this place for forty-eight hours. Believe me when I say I won't botch this up. No way. I may be a lot of things, but I'm not stupid.

I could see the car parked where she said she would be. In the side street, the green GTi was shining. Our old car you see. She didn't get rid of it, just like she didn't get rid of me. You may be surprised. I certainly was. Lizzie would've been well within her rights to do one and disappear back to Scotland, I wouldn't have blamed her. I know what I did was wrong, but she's there waiting. My beautiful woman, my Lizzie. She's all I have left now and I am not going to screw up this time.

Lizzie drives now and surprised me how good she is, given how nervous she used to be. She handles the Golf around the maze that is central London, as if she's done 'the Knowledge.' I couldn't help but notice how good she looks. She's wearing a green knitted dress that clings in all the right places. The high boots I love too. She notices me noticing and grins at me. It's just like the old days. I don't need alcohol and drugs now I'm high on life and on Lizzie.

We hugged as I got into the car. I kissed her face, trying not to notice the scarring. She has covered it up with foundation, too thick, but it does the trick. I know that I have to take things slowly, just like the first time. I wanted to rip off her dress and push my way inside her, but there's no way I'd do that now. I'm no animal. She deserves better than that. She's stood by me and deserves my respect. I've listened well during those boring courses they made me do. It's all about respect.

We pull up at the hostel and I check in while Lizzie waits in the car. I put my bag in the small single room they've put me in and listen as they go through my temporary licence. I assure them I'll be back by eleven tonight, if not earlier. They warn me I'll be tested for alcohol and drugs. No problem I say confidently. The euphoria hasn't left me yet. I hope it never does, I feel on a high that's better than any coke or alcohol.

Lizzie is on her phone when I return. I resist the urge to ask her who she is talking to. She's got new friends from University. I always understood that she was a bright girl, but now she's got a first class honours degree in Psychology from Ruskin, I think. My clever girl. She's talking about doing a masters now whatever that is. I pretend to listen to every word, but my eyes wander down to her legs in those shiny tights. Old urges won't go away I guess.

I expected her to say we'd go somewhere for the day and get to know each other again. Those visits are not the same. You try to talk, but I'm always aware the screws are there, listening to every word. Instead she surprises me by suggesting we go back to the flat. Shocks me in fact. I wasn't expecting that. I tell her I'll go anywhere she wants. She smiles again and pulls away. We're in Leytonstone in forty minutes. She takes out some shopping from the boot, she must have got earlier.

"Steak," she says before I can ask. What a girl.

The place looks smarter than I remember. She chatters away telling me that the couple downstairs have gone.

Someone called Beth lives there now, she is never in though. I'm glad the other two have gone. They didn't see me at my best and bad memories don't fade. I didn't want them giving me a hard time.

We enter the flat and it's immaculate. Freshly decorated, new furniture, nothing to remind me of that last night, thank God. I wait for her to put some music on the CD. That's one memory that I have of her, singing away as she prepares my food. She doesn't though. I look around, I can't even see a CD player.

I don't want to go into the Kitchen, but I do. She unpacks her shopping and I see a bottle of Champagne.

"Oh no Babe, I can't have a drink, you know that." She smiles again.

"I know Terry, but I can." She pops open the cork and I can smell the fizz. It's torture. She pours herself a glass. Well I can toast your homecoming even if you can't. She laughs. I smile too, trying not to think how the drink is tasting as it slips down her throat. She pours me a Fanta, which I suppose will have to do for now.

It all feels weird being here. I wait for her to cook the steak, but instead she grabs me around the waist and pulls me to her and I need little persuading. Soon we're in the bedroom and she peels off her dress to show me some spectacular underwear. I almost came in my pants. We fall on to the bed and soon I'm inside her slippery warmth. I don't think about using a condom and she doesn't mention it either. It's all over within seconds and I apologise to her.

She understands and soon I'm hard again. We spend the next six hours in bed and I'm 'cream crackered.' Lizzie cooks me the steak while I have a little nap. We sit up at the table and chairs that are new. I look at the clock and realise we don't have much time left before I need to get back.

"Don't worry Terry," Lizzie smiles. "We can do it all over again tomorrow."

What a weekend. Better than I could have dreamed about. As I go back through the prison gates I can't wait 'til December. It's all gone great. I haven't slipped up. I've been the model prisoner. Sue Taylor will be disappointed, stupid bitch.

24

Terry
Two months later

I'm still reeling from my weekend release. It's given me a new lease of life and I'm stir crazy desperate to get out to Lizzie and start our lives again. A screw knocks on my cell door and hands me my mail. A letter from Lizzie brings a smile to my face as I pull out the purple headed notepaper. She has got posh since I came in here. It reads:

Dear Terry,

I am missing you so much, since you came home for that weekend. It was so special in so many ways. I have something to tell you Terry. You might need to sit down a minute, it's the best news we could ever have. I am going to have a baby Terry. Our baby. It's due the month before you are released November 18th to be exact. I know they can't be that exact but that's around the date he or she will arrive. Oh my God Terry I am so excited, you cannot know how much this means to me, to us. Or maybe you do. The 'new' Terry seems more understanding and sensitive so you probably do realise how much I have wanted this baby. Your baby.

We have to be careful my love. That nosey Probation Officer must not know, she will be on to social services before we know it. I know all about how it works you see. Our baby will be 'at risk.' They will take it away at a moment's notice if I stay with you. They can just about accept me staying with you after what happened, but a baby? No way.

Don't tell a soul Terry, not your best mate, your cell mate, anyone. Do you understand? I can't visit you now. It won't be long before it will show and the tongues will wag. I will write, but we will have to wait until December until you come home.

I know they will visit you at our flat, but I have a plan. I won't say too much now, but it will be our secret. Our special secret. They won't find baby and we won't say anything until we are ready. If you prove yourself, we will be able to come clean eventually.

I have booked into a new doctor under my maiden name. It won't be traced back. They are not that clever. I don't expect to see your Probation Officer again until you are out. If she wants to come I will put her off. It will be okay Terry I promise you.

I have to go now, I am too emotional to write any more. Take care my love, and be patient. I have been patient over these last three years so you can manage it for a few months surely. I am pretty sure your mail isn't being read. They have too much to do with all the terrorists, but I will still be careful what I say.

Your Lizzie xxxxxxxxxxxxx

My smile is wider now. Oh my God, a baby. I'm going to be a dad. Then the realisation hits me I'll miss the birth. By the time I get out of this shit hole, he or she will already be born. Oh well, I was never good at things like that, squeamish mum would say, but the news has thrown me. She must have planned it, all that sex without protection. The minx. Still, I can't complain. My new family man image will be just perfect. I don't want to share her with a baby if I'm honest, but I've worked through my issues in here. It'll be fine. It'll be better than fine. We couldn't go back to how we were. We need to move forward and having a family is the next logical step. I can see that now.

I'm gutted she won't be visiting though. Apart from Baxter she is the only person I see. Still it's a small price to pay. Life has a funny way of surprising you when you least expect it, doesn't it?

25

Terry
Three months later

Women, I'll never understand them, never in a million years. She promised to write, but apart from the cheques into my canteen to pay for my little luxuries and a quick scribbled note attached, nothing. Nothing to say how it's going. Just chit chat telling me about her dissertation, whatever that is, something to do with college and how she is well. I expected more if the truth be told. I feel like a coiled spring. It's killing me not knowing how the baby's doing and has she had it scanned and that.

She must be nearly five months or so now I think. After Jack, I wondered if she could carry another one. Surely to God she could let me know. All this secrecy, it seems stupid to me. Why would they take our baby? It's not as if I'm a risk to a little one. Keep calm Terry, I'm telling myself. Those anger management courses were useful. Breathe deeply. Why is she doing this? I didn't think it would be like this.

Later that day, I'm handed a letter. From a prisoner who has been out on home leave. I asked him to contact her and find out if she is okay and tell her I'm worried sick.

Dear Terry,

Don't worry my love. Baby and me are fine. Just fine. I have just felt baby kick for the first time, a strong kick. Not as strong as yours, but a kick nevertheless. It's magical. I can't believe that in four months baby will be here and we will be a proper family. I am taking good care of myself and baby. Eating well, sleeping lots and enjoying the miracle.

I can't think too much about you Terry at the moment. To be honest I am pre-occupied with baby and I can't worry about what is happening with you. You can take care of yourself I know that. It won't be long before you will be able to hold baby in your arms and it will all be worth it. I am making arrangements to rent another flat nearby, so baby and me can stay there, when your visits are due. You can say you are living at the flat, but you don't have to be there all the time. You can be with baby and me in our secret place.

Stay strong Terry, and destroy the letter. It won't be long before you are home. The next few months will fly by, and think about what you have to look forward to when you get out.

Your Lizzie xxxxxxxxxxxxxxxxxxxxxxxxxxx

I didn't know what to make of that letter if the truth be known, but part of me felt relieved. I thought she might have done a runner and I'd have no one to come out to, but in my heart I knew she wouldn't. She loves me. She's okay and the baby's okay too. I didn't like the part about not thinking about me though. I didn't like that at all.

26

Terry
Three months later

I'm not good at this waiting game, it's making me ill. I can't sleep, can't think, I just worry, worry, worry. It's torture not hearing from her. Even if I understand why. Well I think I understand. I had a visit today from my Probation Officer Suzanne Taylor. She didn't have a clue what's going on. She asked me if I was preparing for my release. What am I supposed to be doing for fuck's sake? Two and a half months to go. It seems like a fucking lifetime. I couldn't say much to her, I was too angry. My usual good nature replaced with an edginess that won't go away.

My medication calms me down, but even that isn't working right. I keep seeing images of Lizzie, in my mind, getting a passport and packing cases. It's like a nightmare that won't go away. My paranoia had been diagnosed as drug induced, but this paranoia isn't. It's real. Perhaps she's playing with me, perhaps she isn't pregnant at all. Perhaps she is punishing me for what I did to her. My old mum always said that revenge is a dish best served cold. This would be the worst thing she could do, leaving me hanging like this.

I keep having bad thoughts, really bad thoughts. I have to push them away in the dead of night, hearing that old junkie snoring beneath me. I want to scream, really scream. It scares me shitless. I just need to hear something, anything. I don't care about the baby, it's Lizzie I want. I just need to know she still wants me, loves me. Why is she doing this? She could ring, write, anything to put me out of my misery.

I ring her the following day. We agreed not to, in the interest of secrecy. I break the rule and stand in line with my phone card. My heart is pounding so hard I can hardly breathe. The phone rings twice and she answers. She sounds calm; very normal.

"Terry? Why are you ringing me? I thought we agreed."

"I'm sorry babe, I just wanted to hear your voice and know that you're okay." I sigh with the relief of hearing her voice.

"I'm fine Terry, just fine. Everything is fine. I am looking forward to having you home."

Not knowing what to say, I pause. I'm not usually lost for words.

"Got to go now. I am due at the hospital soon to see a friend, you know the one I told you about."

"Soon?" What does she mean?

"Yes. My friend's operation has been brought forward. I'll speak to you soon my love." And with that she hung up.

What the fuck!

27

Terry
Two weeks later

She gets another letter to me. Not through the usual post, but the prison way. I won't say any more. It's not a long letter given I'm due out in a few weeks. I rip into it, like a dying man waiting for his last meal. It's short. Very short.

Dear Terry

I hope you're okay. Sorry about the delay in writing to you my love. I've been busy with my friend. You know Fiona, the one who was having a baby. Poor girl, she has been through the mill, the baby came early, only a few weeks, but she got a bit of a shock. You can imagine. Anyway mum and baby are doing well now, baby weighs nearly six pounds after a couple of weeks of mummy's milk. It's a relief I tell you.

I am looking forward so much to you coming home. The flat is all ready, and I will be waiting for you there. I don't want to come to the prison this time, it's not a nice place to visit and I would rather be here, just waiting. It will all be perfect my love, just perfect.

So hang on in there my love. Count the days down, until we can be together. It's all I have ever wanted. You, my handsome, strong and brave Terry. You have been through so much, I know we can put it behind us and start again. This time it will be different. So different, you won't believe it.

Your Lizzie x

Is she saying what I think she is saying? Our baby is born, safe and well. She doesn't say if it's a boy or a girl. That's weird. Why the hell couldn't she say if I had a son or a daughter? She sounds weird. I can't put my finger on it. The letter asks more questions than it answers. That was deep for me, wasn't it? Still, she's waiting for me, still waiting. That's the main thing. I should be able to rest easy, but I can't. Don't ask me why, I couldn't answer you.

28

Terry
The new start

I thought this day would never come. I feel more nervous than a nun in a brothel. I can't even say why. It's the happiest day of my life, getting out of this shithole. Home to my Lizzie and my new baby. As I sign my licence I realise that I am indeed a lucky man. A very lucky man. I could've been done for manslaughter not GBH. I could've got one of those sentences when I would never know if and when I'd be released.

My lovely Lizzie will be waiting, with our new little one. Girl or boy it doesn't matter. I hope the birth went okay and Lizzie will be up for some action. You hear about these new mums who don't want it for months. I hope she can fit into that underwear she wore last time. Call me selfish if you like, but it's important to a man. She may be a mother now, but she is still my wife.

There's no GTi outside this time. I look anyway in hope. I'll head for the tube, it will be quicker. I've got to report to that bloody woman at the Leytonstone office before I get home. What a pain. I pass an off-licence and look longingly in the window. No not yet. There's too much at stake, I can't go in to that old bag's office smelling of drink.

I remember all the shit I promised. Abstinence is my goal, I told the screws who were running the Alcohol-related Violence Course. Tell them what they want to hear you know. No Jacky D though and no coke, I don't think that they'll go too well with my medication somehow, but a few lagers won't hurt.

The sense of freedom is going to my head. Everything looks bright and fresh, even the coating of snow on the ground. I'm a free man, at long last. I've paid for my crime. It's onward and upward now.

I get off at Leyton and make my way to the Probation Office. Sue keeps me waiting for fifteen minutes, so I feel resentful by the time she does come down and get me. She is in official mode, all licence conditions and warnings. I have to see her every week for bloody years by the sound of it. She arranges a home visit for three days' time. At least I know when the bitch is coming I suppose.

At last I'm out of there and walking along in the winter sun towards my home. I nearly go to mum's, my mind is wandering. The house will be occupied by another family by now I guess and all mum's stuff will be gone. I wonder what Lizzie has done with all her knickknacks. I hope she has kept them, I want something to remember her by.

I consider a quick visit to the Fox. Only for a second or two mind, I don't want to upset her before I even get in the door. At last I'm home. The front door looks shiny as if it's been freshly painted. Perhaps it has in honour of my homecoming. I ring the bell to the flat and wait. Hopping from one foot to another in anticipation.

I can hear her singing as she comes down the final stairs. 'Young hearts run free,' perhaps it's on the radio. *'Self-preservation is what's really going on today. Say I'm gonna turn loose a thousand times a day. Young hearts to yourself be true, don't be no fool when love really don't love you. You'll never be hung up, hung up like my man and me.'*

Her voice is sweeter than ever, as she opens the door. Gone is the green dress, she's wearing some kind of jogging bottoms and a baggy T-shirt. Not quite what I was expecting, but things change. Perhaps she has been up all night with our baby.

Her hair looks straggly too and she's got dark shadows under her eyes. Sleepless nights I suppose. She smiles at me. A strange smile though, not quite matching her eyes.

"Terry." She looks straight at me.

"Lizzie," I say holding out my arms. "I'm home."

29

Terry
The homecoming

I hug her a bit awkwardly. She feels stiff in my arms, not like last time. I breathe in her scent, Obsession by Calvin Klein. At least that hasn't changed. I follow her upstairs. I don't have much to carry up, a small holdall. Mostly the clothes she brought me in prison. She pushes open the door to the flat and I trot behind her desperate to be in my flat again and see my baby.

It is strangely quiet. Like last time, but not what I was expecting. There's no clutter in the living room, it's spotless again and I look around for signs that there is a new baby in the gaff. Nothing.

"How are you babe?" I try not to show any surprise. It feels like her territory now, not mine.

"Okay Terry, but tired. It's hard work you know, looking after Baybe."

"Where is baby?" She's got me at it now. It must have a bloody name for God's sake.

"Sleeping. Baybe likes to sleep a lot."

"Can I see baby? Please."

"Baybe likes quiet Terry, especially in our room. We need a bigger place now."

"We can get a bigger flat babe. Whatever you want."

I was desperate to get into the bedroom, but I didn't move. Lizzie went into the kitchen and brought out a bottle of Champagne.

"We need to toast Baybe, Terry. Surely you can have a drink now?"

God I needed a drink. This was all too much for me. Lizzie was creeping me out. What was going on? She didn't even look like Lizzie. The scars hadn't been covered up with foundation this time. They looked raw on her face. Angry even, as if she had been scratching. She looked a mess.

Lizzie brought the glasses and the bottle and put them on the coffee table. She popped the cork and smiled again. It wasn't a smile I recognised.

We raised our glasses. "To baby," I said.

She smiled again, saying, "to Baybe."

We sat on the sofa, the bubbles went straight to my head. It had been a long time. I was grateful for the lift. This wasn't the homecoming I was expecting, there was something very strange about it all.

Lizzie looked at me. "How do you feel Terry, are you glad to be home?"

"Of course babe, what do you think?"

"I don't know what to think Terry, but let's see how it goes. You can always go to the hostel, if you don't want to be here. At least that's what your Probation Officer said."

"Don't be silly Lizzie, I'm where I want to be." At least I think that's what I said.

We finished the fizz and Lizzie went into the kitchen for another bottle. I was seriously confused now. She knew I shouldn't be drinking and I didn't have the strength to say no. I craved the drink and I didn't know why. It must have been the situation, which was almost sinister.

"Come and see Baybe," said Lizzie suddenly. She literally jumped up off the sofa.

I followed her into the bedroom. It was silent and I could see a small wicker crib in the corner on legs. It was covered in cream lace with a little quilt. I could see baby's face. It was cherub like and peaceful. Too peaceful.

Lizzie went over to the crib and picked baby up. As she held out baby to me, still wrapped in a knitted blanket I could see that there was no life there.

"Oh my fucking God, what have you done to our baby?"

30

Terry

It took a few seconds for me to realise that baby wasn't dead. Baby had never lived, in order to die. Baby was a doll. A very lifelike doll, but a doll nonetheless. She had been created to look like a newborn. Very realistic, but still a doll. What the hell was Lizzie playing at?

"Lizzie, it's a fucking doll. What's going on?"

I will never forget that laugh. It was like nothing I have ever heard before or since. A shriek with an underlying cackle. A mad woman's laugh. Many things were going through my head. Had she had a phantom pregnancy and then bought this thing as a substitute. Had she miscarried again? I couldn't think straight.

"Oh Terry I didn't think you would take it so badly."

She was still laughing hysterically.

"Take what badly?" I was still reeling.

"It's a joke Terry, a joke." She continued to laugh rocking back and forth. "Do you remember jokes?"

I was getting angry now, I could feel the familiar signs.

"I know you didn't want a baby, you want it to be just us. I thought you would get it." She looked puzzled at my reaction.

"A joke?" I looked at her again. "Are you for real?"

She stopped laughing. "Oh Terry, you're not angry are you? I thought you would be pleased you don't have to share me with anyone."

She was deadly serious now and unhinged by the look of it. Why hadn't I seen it before?

For the first time in my life I didn't know how to play it. I really didn't. My whole world was spinning on its axle. The last few months, all the anxiety and stress, the worry and the paranoia. I could have killed her there and then, but I didn't want to spend the rest of my days back in prison. She wasn't worth it. My licence said I had to be here, so here I would be.

"Okay babe," I said, "I get it, joke over."

"Oh Terry I knew you would see the funny side. You didn't want to come home to a house full of baby now did you? You like your home comforts too much."

We went back into the living room and she was acting as if nothing much had happened.

"But what about the letters, the not visiting me? That wasn't very nice babe."

"Oh Terry, I got a job, singing on a cruise ship. I knew you wouldn't like it much. So I thought of Baybe, to stop you getting jealous Hun."

It was too much to take in. I gulped at my Champagne. "Me, jealous Lizzie? No way babe."

She went into the kitchen singing 'Too busy thinking 'bout my baby. I ain't got time for nothing else.' One of my mum's favourites. She wasn't right. I could see that, but I didn't know what to do about it.

She cooked dinner and I finished the wine. She gave me a can of Stella, while I waited for her to dish up.

"Your favourite babe, Lasagne." We ate our food in silence. I drank my beer.

"Do you mind if I go and see the lads in the Fox?" I had to get out of there.

"Course not Terry. It's what you do best."

31

Terry

Two days since my release and things in the flat weren't getting any better. Sue Taylor was due at eleven and I had told Lizzie to put baby away in the cupboard. She obliged, but wasn't happy about it.

"No one puts Baybe in a corner." She pulled a face, then the upset turned to laughter in an instant. I was intending to ask Sue if she could find me somewhere else to live if I got the chance, but I didn't want to jeopardise my licence though. There was no way I was going back to prison. Not for Lizzie, 'Baybe' or anyone else.

I decided to say nothing. I had cleared away any evidence of beer or alcohol and warned Lizzie to be on her best behaviour. I'd spent the last two nights in the pub, but Lizzie had been asleep when I got back to the flat and I slept on the sofa. It was like living with an alien. Except it was one that looked and sounded like my Lizzie. She was singing all the time, even when I was sleeping. Her choice of songs, varied but were all of the same theme. 'I'm sick and tired of you, little darling,' by Merle Travis was the favourite, followed by 'Who's sorry now?' by Connie Francis. To Terry it was torture of the worst kind. Then when Sue was due, Lizzie decided she was going out.

"Won't she want to talk to you?" I asked.

"I don't know," said Lizzie innocently. "Just tell her I'm at college and that she can ring me if she wants." And with that she went.

Sue looked around the flat and looked at me. Asking all the usual questions, how was it going, how was I getting on with Lizzie. I used my skills to lie convincingly, I hope. It was a skill of mine. I described the meals she had made me, how glad she was to see me and how I was grateful for her help and support. It seemed to work. She gave me an appointment to see her at the office for the following week. I couldn't wait to see the back of her.

I couldn't leave here at the moment though, not without it jeopardising everything. I had to stay with the mad woman and hope that it would be okay. I couldn't raise a hand to her though, no matter what she did, I knew that.

Lizzie returned a few hours later. She had bags with her, she had obviously been shopping. Where was she getting the money? She was a poor student. Oh yes, she had worked on the cruise liner for a few months, that must have paid well.

"Terry do you realise what day it is tomorrow?"

I had lost track of the days, it was all getting too bizarre.

32

Lizzie

It was the anniversary of their marriage eight years ago. Lizzie had planned a special night and told Terry he could go to the pub, but he had to be back by nine. She was going to cook a special dinner. It was all planned. She would make a roast, like the one she made on the night it all went wrong. This time it wouldn't go wrong. Terry was already slipping back to his old ways. She hadn't expected anything different.

Baybe had spooked him. Lizzie guessed that it would. It was comforting to see him unable to work the situation out, above all as he so liked to be in control. Lizzie had spooked him so much, he didn't even want sex with her, so that was a bonus. She guessed that Tina at the pub was obliging him in that department. She hoped so, just as long as he left her alone.

Lizzie wondered if she actually was going mad. All those years to think about Terry and what he had done to her, to Jack, to poor little Frankie and to anyone who he came into contact with. He was toxic. The worse thing about it all was he thought he could fool everyone, Lizzie, his Probation Officer Sue Taylor and the authorities.

Lizzie put on some music. She had re-installed the CD player for the time being. She had a pile of CDs that Terry would hate, but that didn't matter. 'Sisters were doing it for themselves.' She laughed out loud, which sounded weird even to her, as it was an empty room.

She liked unnerving Terry, he had spent most of his sentence thinking she was the doting wife waiting at home. It hadn't been hard to visit once a month and keep up the pretence. Lizzie hadn't realised what a great actress she was until Terry had gone into prison. She should have applied to RADA.

It had taken her years, but she had realised that not only was Terry incredibly sadistic, cruel and narcissistic, he was also thick. Okay he was streetwise and savvy in some ways, but he was thick. He could use cunning better than a fox and lie well enough to win medals, but he didn't understand women in the way he thought he did. He was a player, but he didn't know the game. He'd thought he could break her, break her spirit and leave her in a place she could never leave.

Lizzie understood now why women stay with these vile men. They are so worn down, they can't fight back and it becomes a vicious circle. If Terry hadn't gone to prison, she'd be in the same position herself. He'd chosen his victim well. She had been a gullible young girl when she was taken in by Terry's charms, his warmth and his helpfulness. He alienated her from her parents and friends and she ended up having no one in her life other than him.

If it hadn't been for his mother, she wouldn't have had a soul to talk to. She thought of Mrs Mac. Had she loved her 'Terence' too much? Probably, but then again she was a victim too. First at the hands of Terry's father, he wrote the Macintosh rule book and then her only child picked up where his father left off. Women were second class citizens whose primary functions were sex and food. It. The 'sins of the fathers' went deeper than that though, Lizzie had fathomed out that much.

She peeled potatoes, carrots and broccoli for the dinner. She had bought a leg of lamb to roast and some rosemary. Let Terry enjoy his last meal, she thought without a sense of irony. She did her hair and put on a nice dress. He might even think she was up for Terry's favourite recreation. That would be funny too.

Terry turned up an hour late, she knew he would. He had decided that he wouldn't let Lizzie dictate to him when he should be home. After seven pints of Stella, he had made a few decisions in the pub. This situation, Lizzie behaving like some weirdo, couldn't go on any longer. Chiefly the not sharing a bed with him.

He'd tried it on with Tina in the pub, she used to be up for it without a problem, but she told him where to go. She'd heard what he did to Lizzie and the little dog, she didn't want a man like that near her, the evil bastard. Terry's paranoia had heightened further with the feeling that other people were giving him the kiss-off too.

He was ready to have it out with Lizzie. As he entered the flat, he could smell the lamb. 'Oh well she's made an effort.' Lizzie came to the door to greet him. She had a red Lycra dress on, tight in all the right places. Perhaps it wouldn't be a bad night after all. He went to give her a hug and she didn't recoil. He sat down at the table and she poured him a beer. 'This was good.'

As Lizzie served up his dinner, he smiled at her. His winning smile that he hoped would work and all this nonsense would stop. Lizzie looked at her husband. He was still handsome, but tired around the eyes. His waistline had grown in prison and the beer he'd been drinking since his release gave him a bloated look. He wasn't much of a catch anymore.

They ate their food and Terry drank more. Lizzie wondered how much he could take after a three year gap. He was slurring his words now and missing his mouth with his fork. Liz stood up and went to the kitchen for dessert. She had put on a smoochy CD and 'Unbreak my heart' was playing in the background. She slipped out to the hallway and quietly opened the front door.

Terry was slumped back in the seat. He must have had a skinful in the pub, Lizzie decided. She thought he would. So much for his promise of abstinence. She remembered all the letters he had sent from prison. All meaningless, she thought. He would say anything if he thought it would get him what he wanted.

She sang along with the record, Rose Royce's 'Love don't live here anymore.'

"Come on Terry, let's have a dance."

"Okay babe," he stood up, swaying a little.

He grabbed her around the waist and they started a slow smooch. He could smell her perfume and as he nuzzled into her neck, she led him towards the front door.

"Where are we going babe? He was puzzled, but she felt so warm, so soft. He held on to her.

The doorway that led to the stairs was open. Terry wondered for a moment if he'd forgotten to close it. He wanted to ask why again, as they passed through it and out onto the landing, but his thought processes were moving slower than his feet.

Lizzie moved swiftly now, holding Terry around the neck as they danced, she used all the strength she had to push him face forward down the stairs.

Lizzie enjoyed the sound as his face hit the large and very solid newel post at the bottom of the flight. Images flashed through her mind, of baby Jack as she held his lifeless waxy body in her arms after she had delivered him and his beautiful, perfect little face. The sound of little Frankie as Terry hurled him down the same stairs, the life force snapped out of him, as Terry laughed maniacally.

She looked at the figure of her husband lying crumpled up where the stairs meet the lower landing. He didn't make a sound either. Was that a good sign she wondered? She walked back inside the flat and phoned 999. She was lucky that there was nobody in downstairs to report the noise, or the crime. But what would they have reported? There had been no argument, or screams.

The Police arrived quickly. Terry McIntosh was on licence and he was a nutter. They were taking no chances, but it was his missus who had rung, saying they had a row and he had tried to kill her.

When they saw Lizzie sobbing on the sofa, the officers' hearts went out to her, the poor woman, Terry was just out of prison after a three year stretch. She told PC West how she had cooked him a lovely dinner, 'it was our anniversary,' which started off a fresh bout of sobbing. Terry said he wouldn't drink any more, but he went to the pub and brought back more cans. He was like an animal, he wanted to have sex with me in the living room. Her dress was ripped. She had some bruising around her eye that would soon swell.

I told him to get out and I opened the door. Oh my God Officers, he went for me again, but he was that drunk he lost his footing and the next thing he was toppling down the stairs. The other officer, was still taking Terry's pulse as he called for an ambulance.

"He's not dead," he shouted up the stairs. Lizzie's heart almost stopped. But he had to be dead. He must be dead. She wanted her new life and she wanted the insurance payout. He had to be dead.

33

Terry

W here the hell was I? Not back in prison please God? It was too bright white and neon to be prison. Lights were shining in my face. What the fuck? Then darkness again. Blissful darkness. I could hear voices, talking about me as if I was dead. Was this it? Was this death I wondered? The bright light was a good sign then. Was I in heaven already? Wait a minute, hell more likely, in my case and I'll have more in common with Satan's gang. I was joking, but shitting myself inside.

I couldn't feel panic. It just felt as though it was all out of my control. I couldn't move, it was like a dream sequence when you can't wake up in time, that horrible feeling as you try your hardest to move. Your mind has woken up, but your body hasn't. Do you know what I mean?

Time meant nothing anymore. I couldn't tell you how long it all went on for. Minutes, hours, days, weeks, was I in a coma? I could think, but I couldn't speak. I could see, but I couldn't move. It was as if I had become a floating brain, you know like that Steve Martin film. What has happened to me? Where's Lizzie?

Then I saw her. She was blurry, but she sat down next to me and held my hand. Maybe I've been in an accident. I could hear her sobbing. It upset me to be truthful. I tried to comfort her, but I couldn't do a thing. Only my eyes could communicate. I tried to look at her properly. Tears dripped down on to my hand.

"Oh Terry," she was saying, "oh Terry why couldn't you just die, you fucking bastard."

It wasn't what I was expecting at all.

Someone in a white uniform came up behind her.

"Mrs McIntosh, we need to take Terry down for a 'brain scan.' Terry has 'Locked-in Syndrome,' we know that, but we need to ascertain the full extent of his condition. You are welcome to go and get a coffee until we bring him back up."

Then Lizzie said a strange thing.

"Will he live, Doctor?"

"It's too early to be a hundred percent sure, but his condition is stable and he is young and strong enough to live for years."

She turned to look at me, but her eyes didn't match the words that came from her mouth.

"Oh good, Doctor, that's a relief."

As she walked away, one of the nurses or whatever they were, said to the doctor, "she is so devoted isn't she? She's been here all day every day for the last week. She must really love him."

I couldn't feel my heart any more, but if I had, it would have gone cold. Lizzie had tried to kill me, but I was still alive. My memory was coming back, bit by bit. Had she pushed me, or had I fallen. I couldn't be sure, but I could be sure she wanted me dead. I would have to fight with every bone in my body to stay alive. The problem was I couldn't feel any bone in my body. That was a real problem.

34

Lizzie

T erry was coming home. Not the same Terry who had left the flat when Lizzie had hoped and prayed it would be in a box. It wasn't even the same flat. Lizzie had had to rent the bottom one from Sanjay, so Terry and his wheelchair could get in and out. It was unoccupied and Sanj was sympathetic to Terry's plight, so the process wasn't too difficult. She could just about get the chair up and down the steps into the flat, but it took all her strength and energy. Lizzie wasn't too worried about that though, apart from his hospital appointments she had no intention of taking him anywhere.

Lizzie was still in a state of shock. Shock that Terry had survived the fall and all the plans she had made had dissolved and to her annoyance, he'd lived on. He couldn't move though, so he could never hurt her again. His brain stem trauma was severe enough to ensure that he had no mobility, at all. He couldn't speak either, which was lucky, but he could look or stare in a way that made Lizzie very uncomfortable.

The doctors had done their best, but apart from physiotherapy and regular check-ups, there was little more that they could do. He could move his head and eat and drink slowly, if he was fed, but his vocal chords could only make inaudible noises. The speech therapist believed he might be able to learn how to speak again. Lizzie hoped not, not in the time she would be with him anyway.

Plan 'B' was harder to execute and she needed time to think. For the foreseeable, she was stuck with Terry.

Lizzie had other much more important things to do with her time. She sat him in the corner of the room facing the TV. She put it on a shopping channel and left him to watch.

"Look Terry, cleaning products, your favourite."

When she came back three hours later Terry hadn't moved. His catheter bag was full and he looked puzzled. Then he scowled his special scowl, at least with his eyes. She gave him his water as directed by the doctor. Okay, it was supposed to be every hour, but that wasn't going to happen. He wouldn't dehydrate. He drank the water, some of it dribbling down his chin. Lizzie didn't think she was cut out to be a nurse. She was already dreading dealing with his other bodily functions. Hopefully it wouldn't be for long.

Terry was looking intently at Lizzie. She went in to the bedroom and came back with Baybe.

"Come on Terry, Baybe isn't making as much fuss as you. And don't look at me like that!"

Terry's head was moving now in anger, not much, but she could sense his agitation.

"Baybe hates Terry. It's sad, but Baybe knows what you did to mummy." Sitting back in the chair Lizzie cradled Baybe. "We have all the time in world now Terry to make up for those years when you were in prison. When we couldn't talk."

Terry's puzzled look returned.

"Baybe knows what mummy did when you were in prison, but she will never tell, will you Baybe?"

Terry spluttered again his eyes darting back and forth.

"Baybe knows that mummy didn't like having an empty bed didn't she?" Lizzie smiled down at Baybe. She was going to have such fun.

35

Terry

You can't imagine how it fucking feels, not being able to move. I want to die. I want to join my mum somewhere else other than this place. This flat with this woman who calls herself my wife. The woman who said she loved me is now treating me worse than an animal. She's turned raving psycho. There should be men in white coats here to take her away to a nut-house. It would be for her own good. And mine!

It's like a torture that'll never end. She's supposed to be looking after me, but she leaves me on my own for hours, either with the telly or that fucking doll to stare at.

Can you imagine how that feels? No I don't suppose you can. She's become an evil bitch from hell and she's enjoying it, I can tell. Tell me, what sane, normal person could get any pleasure from mistreating a defenceless human being?

I don't know, but I know this much, she's a dead woman walking. When I get out of this chair I'll kill her. Properly kill her.

36

Lizzie

L izzie was bored with Terry now. She had spent the afternoon singing with Baybe, all the songs he particularly hated. She then gave him his dinner, a hot curry that burnt his mouth. She had to be careful though, she didn't want to be accused of abusing him. Not that anyone would blame her after what he'd put her though.

No, she was cleverer than that. She liked to talk to Terry. It was fun to tell him what kind of person he was. Baybe liked to tell Terry too, through Lizzie of course and the biggest joy was, he couldn't answer back. She thought though a couple of times that Terry might move, such was his will to do so. Can anger be the strongest of all emotions ever she wondered? If so, perhaps Terry would walk again someday?

Lizzie had been shopping. Her parcels had arrived from the 'special website' she had found a few days before. It was a quick delivery. Lizzie was excited as she told Terry what she had bought.

"Look Terry you can look just like Baybe."

She held up a big blue Babygro with a hood. He tried to move again, making faint groaning noise in his throat, it seemed like a muffled scream.

"Stop that noise Terry, you haven't seen the rest yet."

She held up a big blue rattle, baby bottle and some adult nappies. "Well Terry, I thought since you have to wear the nappies, you might as well have the rest of the outfit to go with them. You will look so cute."

Terry was dribbling and trying to growl. She remembered the night he'd really growled, before he put the pan of hot fat over her. It spurred Lizzie on, as she dressed him in the outfit. She took some pictures with her phone and showed them to him.

"Look Terry that's you and so cute. Baybe wants one the same as yours now."

She put some music on, a compilation she had made of songs with the word 'baby' in the title. There were quite a few. She danced round Terry holding Baybe and singing along for a good hour or so. Exhausted she lay down on the sofa holding Baybe up in front of her and kissing her face. Terry was closing his eyes to the cruel show, but it mattered little. He could still hear her even if he couldn't see her. How much of this he could take before he went totally insane? The fact was that no one would ever know. Terry was now in hell. A hell of his own making.

Lizzie performed the duties as instructed in the hospital. She fed him, gave him water, changed his colostomy bags and washed him. After a week she was running out of things to do at playtime. She didn't want to look at him in the corner any more. He was still a malevolent figure even though he couldn't move. There was only so much she could do. Every night she ate his favourite meals, then fed him porridge sometimes with salt and sometimes with sugar. He spat it out at first, but he didn't want to die, she knew that. He thought he would get out of there one day. Her Terry was a fighter, but he wouldn't win this fight.

She dressed in her favourite underwear and when Baybe had been put to bed, she would lie in front of him and play with herself. Terry's squirming would increase and she liked to see him get more and more agitated. She told him that she was glad he hadn't died. Baybe was glad he hadn't died too. They wouldn't have the fun they were having now if he had. Baybe likes fun, she told him and so does mummy.

The following afternoon she was expecting a visit from Sue Taylor. Sue didn't need to worry about Terry any more, he couldn't hurt anyone now and apparently she was going to lower his risk. That made her giggle.

Lizzie spoke to Terry about the upcoming visit.

"Terry what would you like to wear for Sue, we want you to look smart for your Probation Officer, don't we? You can tell her what you have been doing." At this point she burst out laughing again. "What have you been doing Terry? Apart from shitting in your bag? You can tell her about that. Baybe doesn't shit in a bag, Baybe's clean."

She held Baybe's face up to Terry as he tried to move his head away.

"Don't do that Terry, or I will put you in the Christmas jumper again. I promise you. I don't care if it is April."

37

Lizzie

Terry felt as if he was going to explode, or implode internally. It was more than anyone should have to bear. At two o'clock there was a knock on the door and Lizzie ushered Sue Taylor into the living room. She explained to her they had moved flats so Terry could get in and out.

"We're always out and about, aren't we Terry"

She smiled at him in what Sue felt to be quite a sinister way. Terry couldn't speak, only make sounds and Sue couldn't work out one sound from another. She couldn't believe it was the same man.

Lizzie told Sue, that it was best for Terry to be out and getting some fresh air and stimulation. Sue looked at Terry. His head was to one side and he was wearing Tottenham Hotspur football kit. A strange choice of outfit, she thought looking at his 'carer.' Lizzie smiled at her.

"It's hard work Sue, but I have to look after him. I wouldn't let anyone else do it. Whatever he has done, he's still my man."

Sue wondered what really had happened on the night of their anniversary. She wouldn't have blamed Lizzie if she *had* pushed him down the stairs, although it didn't look as though she had, according to the police. Terry had been drinking, a lot. His blood/alcohol level was five times the legal limit to drive. So much for abstinence thought Sue. He couldn't stay off the booze, or leave his wife alone, not even for a few days. She hadn't had too much optimism about his release anyway, but this was sad seeing him like this. Sue asked Lizzie to let her know if there was any change in Terry's condition. She also wondered how long it would be before Lizzie put him into care. There's only so much a woman could take and Lizzie had taken more than most.

"Come on you Spurs," laughed Lizzie after his Probation Officer had gone.

"I've got you another new outfit Terry. Wait 'til you see it." She unwrapped another parcel. "You can get anything on the internet these days Terry."

It was a green dress, like the one she'd worn for the weekend he'd come home.

"Shall we try it my lovely Terry?" She had also purchased a wig and some boots. Lizzie and Baybe had great fun, making him up and putting him in the outfit.

"Baybe likes your dress Terry."

Lizzie had bought a big full length mirror so Terry could look at himself. He was trying desperately to shake the wig off, but he couldn't move it at all.

"You're useless Terry. Look at you. Or should I call you Lizzie? You look like Lizzie don't you? Well, an uglier Lizzie. What was it you used to call me Terry? Oh I remember, a rubbish cook, not a patch on your mum, a crap shag and a worthless 'see you next Tuesday.' All those little words of love will stay forever in my heart Terry, do you know that?"

The following day Lizzie and Baybe returned with a toy dog in soft plastic. It was a model resembling the little dog Terry had killed.

"Look Terry it's poor little Frankie. Well it's a rubber Frankie anyway. Don't look Baybe."

She turned Baybe's face away as she pushed the dog into Terry's anus.

"Aww Terry does it hurt babe? Probably not eh?"

Terry could feel his internal organs, but he still couldn't move. As Lizzie twisted the dog around, she reminded Terry of the time when she was pregnant. He'd pushed her onto the floor and forced her to have anal sex. Lizzie's eyes were wild as she forced the dog as high as it would go, before it needed to be surgically removed. Terry was screwing up his eyes to look at her in the most menacing way he could and he was frothing at the mouth. Lizzie pulled away and picked up Baybe.

"Come on my little one, let's go and leave nasty Terry on the floor tonight."

The next morning, he was lying in the same position and Lizzie laughed as she picked up the stuff from the floor. She gave him his breakfast while he was still naked. It wasn't cold in the flat, so he wouldn't die. She had given him milk in the bottle, so she washed up the blue teat.

She liked the feeling of his dependence on her. Terry needed her now just to live. "Blue for a boy, eh Terry? What shall we do today? I know, Baybe wants to dance don't you Baybe?"

She went to the CD player and Terry's heart sank. 'Oh God not more baby songs, or worse still, the feminist anthems. It was bad enough hearing her fucking singing.'

There was a knock on the door. Who was that thought Lizzie, no one comes here. It was Baxter, Terry's old mate from school and the Fox. He was still huge with his beer belly hanging over his jeans and just as unattractive as ever. She had tried to like Baxter, he meant well, but he had always looked up to Terry. To Baxter, with his looks and physique, he was a God. Still he wasn't impressed when Terry was arrested and he didn't condone hitting women. Lizzie knew he liked her, but they had little to say to each other.

"Hi Baxter," said Lizzie brightly. "How are you? I didn't realise you knew we had moved."

"The woman upstairs told me," he replied. Evidently there was a new tenant on the middle floor. "How's Tel? Can I see him?"

"Oh Baxter, I'm changing him just now. You know what I mean? I'm sure Terry wouldn't want you to see him like that."

Baxter was already backing away. He couldn't visualise it and didn't want to. He'd seen Terry at the hospital once or twice, but hadn't known what to say.

"Look I don't want him to think I have forgotten him okay? Tell him I came round and I'll come back sometime."

"I will tell him Baxter." Terry was trying to make a noise from the lounge, it sounded like a strangled growl.

"What's that noise?"

"Oh it's a new puppy Baxter, to replace Frankie, the one Terry killed. My little Binky. It was Terry's idea."

Baxter nodded. It must have been before the accident. God, he wouldn't want Terry's life at any price.

"See you around Lizzie," he said, knowing he probably wouldn't.

"Okay Baxter, take care." Lizzie closed the door and turned back into the room where Terry was lying.

"You're in trouble now Terry. Baybe told me you were making a noise. Baybe doesn't like Baxter coming round here."

A few hours later, when Terry had his 'bath' with Lizzie and Baybe, he wished more than ever that he was dead.

And so the long weeks continued. Lizzie was running out of ideas to inflict more misery on Terry. He had served his purpose in terms of retribution and entertainment. Lizzie wondered how she could put an end to it all. Not another fall down the stairs that would be too obvious. It would have to be outside the flat.

She spent a few days looking for the best place. Finally she found it. A small hardware shop on the corner of the main high road, with a slope just enough to let the wheelchair roll on to a main road. The timing needed to be perfect. She dressed up for the occasion and washed her hair.

She was going to tell Terry before they went out, but thought it would be a cruelty too far. Anyway he didn't have a 'life' as it was, so he would be better off dead. So would Lizzie, financially, emotionally, physically and sexually. Just like the aspects of domestic abuse she'd studied all those years ago.

It was an unfortunate 'accident.' Terry's chair was struck by a white Mercedes Sprinter van and this time he didn't survive. No one had seen what happened and the poor driver was distraught. Lizzie was hysterical, repeating over and over.

"I must have forgotten to put the brake on, when I went into the shop. I was only going in for a new washing up bowl, so I could do Terry's feet."

There was a lot of debate about it at the local Police Station. Some thought she might have done it, others didn't think she was capable of it. There was no proof and Lizzie was a match for all the questions. She had convinced the coroner, who didn't blame Lizzie; she was a grieving widow after all. 'Accidental Death,' was the official verdict.

Sue Taylor wondered what had happened. Had it been a terrible accident? Was Lizzie the best actress she had ever encountered? Had she planned it all? Sue couldn't decide, but it was one less 'high risk' case for her to worry about, she'd forget about it now. No one would miss Terry McIntosh, apart from his wife, if it hadn't been an act. Was it 'an act of charity' maybe?

38

Lizzie

Lizzie walked slowly from the Coroner's office. Thank God that was over. She was free now. There would be no come back. No one to point the finger. She had already bought a new flat in Chiswick, a nice area of West London. She had her Master's Degree and she had the Insurance Company's money in the bank, including a big pay out for his first injuries and she had spent little of it on his care.

Terry's body had been donated to science. Perhaps they would open up his brain and find out what had made him the monster he was, or that he became. She had wondered about nature versus nurture. In psychological terms anyway. Was Terry born evil?

Things he'd done as a child suggested that he was a psychopath, who would've done something terrible whatever happened. Lizzie knew about the terrible violence at football matches that he seemed to get away with. One of his alleged victims had brain damage, but Terry was never convicted.

She couldn't feel sad for her husband or what she had done. She felt sad for the girl she had once been. The good girl who believed in love and in Terry, trusting he'd look after her with respect. That was all she had wanted.

She got on a bus back to Leytonstone. She had rung her landlord Sanjay with whom she had been on very good terms with, over the years. Especially the last few years. She'd been lonely and he hadn't met Mrs Right yet. He helped her through it and allowed her to rent the two flats cheaply, because she was a friend with benefits.

Lizzie had already cleaned out the bottom flat where she had lived with Terry for a while. She was leaving all the furniture in both flats for Sanjay. He could now rent them furnished if he wanted to, she didn't want to see any of it ever again. She wanted a fresh start and could afford to buy new.

Lizzie opened the door to the top flat. She could hear Sonja, her Polish saviour singing to herself. Some kind of lullaby she guessed.

"Is everything okay?" Sonja asked as Lizzie opened the door. Lizzie nodded, the relief showing on her face. She would have hugged Sonja, but she was holding Angel wrapped in a papoose as she rocked her.

Lizzie took her from Sonja's arms and kissed her rosebud lips gently. She smelt like all babies should smell. Soap and innocence, a heady combination. Angel stirred and looked up into her mother's eyes. Her bright blue eyes widened when she saw the most important person in her life. She could smell Lizzie's milk from ten yards away. "Time for a feed," smiled her mum.

Lizzie sat and fed her while Sonja finished packing the two small bags they were taking with them. Personal items, passports, photos, some CDs and the like. Sonja put the prison letters from Terry into a black sack.

"All rubbish?" She asked, looking at Lizzie.

"Yes. All rubbish. Come on, let's get out of here."

Lizzie shut the door behind her and put the keys through the door. She carried the infant downstairs in the papoose, Sonja followed with the bags.

Before opening the outer door to the street, Lizzie kissed Sonja long and softly on the lips, trying not to squeeze her little Angel who had fallen into peaceful slumber.

We hope this book throws up some interesting discussion and debate.

If you have enjoyed it, please tell your friends, or be kind enough to write a review on which ever website you favour.

Your comments, reviews and feedback are always welcomed by Beatrice, at this email address:

Beatrice@BeatriceJames.com

Or tweet to: **@obilium**

Should you wish to be kept informed about future publications, send a short note to the above email address, or tweet to @obilium.

Volume 3 – Act 2 of **THE RETRIBUTION FANTASIES** series will be published, during Spring 2015.

Titled: **THE COLDEST DISH** – It tells the story of a life with a controlling and cruel-hearted Celebrity Chef.

11510226R00082

Printed in Great Britain
by Amazon.co.uk, Ltd.,
Marston Gate.